"I want to have you, right here on the plane," Valerie murmured in my ear as she moved her hand under the blanket and began unfastening my pants.

My head was swirling. I felt good. Very good indeed. She wanted to have me, right here, first class. I had had my share of adventurous sex . . . but on an airplane? God only knew how many miles up we were, racing across the sky in a silver bullet, surrounded by an odd assortment of midnight travelers, including the lady with the bun. I shifted my head slightly, trying to get a better idea of who was actually awake. The plane was dark, quiet. Who would know? Valerie's cool fingers moved down onto the smooth skin of my stomach, trying to sneak their way deeper and deeper toward my thick nest of hair.

"Pull them down. Pull your pants down right now."

PLAYERS

ROBBI SOMMERS

The Naiad Press, Inc.
1992

Printed in the United States of America on acid-free paper
First Edition
2nd Printing September 1992

Edited by Christine Cassidy
Cover design by Pat Tong and Bonnie Liss
(Phoenix Graphics)
Typeset by Sandi Stancil

Library of Congress Cataloging-in-Publication Data

Sommers, Robbi, 1950—
Players / by Robbi Sommers
p. cm.
ISBN 0-941483-73-8
I. Title.
PS3569.065335P48 1990
813'.54—dc20 90-6237
CIP

About the Author

Robbi Sommers was born in Cincinnati, Ohio in 1950. She currently lives in Santa Rosa, California, where she divides her time between dental hygiene and motherhood. Even so, it is rumored that she frequents the most exotic of worlds.

My heartfelt thanks to those who stood by my side
And helped me face the dark.
Marisa, Susie, Loraine and Jean.
And special gratitude to my muse, who knows quite well who she is . . .

To Ruby . . .
My sister, my shadow, my mirror.

PLAYERS

ROBBI SOMMERS

Chapter 1

Last Wednesday night, I was cleaning out my closet, I had just come home from a major shopping spree — I mean *a major spree* — because I needed a new look and decided that I was finally willing to clean out some of the clothes I hadn't worn for a while. These are the kind of things a woman will do when she's either falling in love or her heart's been broken.

I made a pile of the "give-away clothes." I was proud of myself for having had the strength to weed out garments I hadn't worn for years. I carried the pile out to a box in the garage. I figured I'd toss them in there until I had a chance to unload the stuff.

By the time I reached the garage, I found myself emotionally involved yet again with three quarters of the things in my "give-away pile" (or what only moments before had been the "give-away pile"). Now I was just referring to it as "the pile."

I placed the clothes on the work table, sorting through them one last time, just to be sure. The remaining scarf and ripped jeans that I finally decided I didn't want were now the new, "re-evaluated give-away pile." Three pair of pants, four sweaters, and six blouses were now the "back-to-the-closet pile."

It's odd how that seems to work. I hadn't worn anything in the "back-to-the-closet pile" in a couple of years, but all of a sudden they seemed . . . I don't know, as if they shouldn't be in the "give-away pile."

I took the now, shall we say, "more abbreviated give-away pile" and walked over to the storage box. Just as I was getting ready to drop the stuff in, I saw, at the bottom of the box, lying on a stack of old papers, a letter.

I hadn't been through that box in quite some time, but it was strange to see the letter, considering it was not like me to hold on to that type of memorabilia. Needless to say, I was somewhat intrigued.

The envelope was not postmarked. The name "Markie" was scribbled across it in my own handwriting. Markie. Now there was a woman I hadn't allowed myself to think about in a long time. The only woman who had ever gotten in close enough to tear my heart to shreds.

I felt a small wave of darkness pass through me. That shadow was just a momentary sensation, moving through me and then disappearing. Good. I could finally think of Markie and be okay. What was it, a year and a half now?

I took the letter and placed it along with the scarf and the torn jeans, on top of the "back-to-the-closet pile." I figured I might *need* those jeans one day. The scarf was for good measure.

Returning to the bedroom, I tossed the "back-to-the-closet pile" next to the "new clothes pile" and then lay down on the bed, still clutching the letter I had written to Markie so many months ago.

I remembered writing that letter. It was the night I found out Markie had betrayed me. That kind of thing had never happened to me. *I* was usually the one hurting someone else. I was unable "to refrain from taking new lovers during every relationship I had ever had," a weakness until I became involved with Markie.

I smelled the letter, wondering if there was any scent left from the perfume that I had soaked the stationery in before writing the note. Truthfully, if I had sent the letter off to Markie at the time — and if she had been smoking a cigarette when she opened it — it probably would have burst into flames. The paper had been drenched in cologne.

I had been trying to make some sort of romantic

final plea, as if smelling the fragrance I wore as she read my "please don't leave me" note could possibly have made a difference.

I inhaled deeply. Was I imagining that light fragrant mist rising up from the open envelope? Not possible that the scent could still be clinging, rather insistently at that, I'm certain, but I felt a shiver race through me anyway because it *seemed* as though I could detect a hint of the fragrance I wore for only Markie . . . and haven't worn since.

I lifted the flap, pulled out the letter, and began to read. I tried to be matter-of-fact, but realized that each word I read upset me, as if pushing a needle embedded deep in my heart for over a year.

I exhaled slowly, thinking that I shouldn't put myself through the unneeded ritual of reading this letter, bringing up all those buried feelings. But I can't imagine one person who wouldn't have done the same under these circumstances. Like that pile of give-away clothes, there might be a certain honor or respectability in the attempt to create the pile, but inevitably, they end up back in the closet.

Feelings, no matter how old, are never that simple to dispose of. There's a certain compulsion to sort through them in a *pretense* of cleaning them out (as though one could possibly replace them with newer emotions!), and then quietly put them back in the very place they have always been.

I suppose that's why I thought to read the letter. It was like carrying the torn jeans, no longer usable, back to the closet, not wanting to risk what I *could* lose if I trashed them. This letter represented feelings I didn't care to carry around anymore. Yet finding the letter created an uncontrollable urge to take those emotions out and sort through them once again. And more importantly, I felt that reading the letter might serve to remind me how I had come to the place I am today. I wanted those tiny stabs in my heart to reinforce my decision *never* to fall back into being the person I had been before Markie. I reread the letter slowly, carefully, as if trying to control the piercing of that sharp needle:

> MARKIE —
> HOW COULD YOU HAVE *EVER EVER* DONE THIS TO ME?
> I AM PRAYING THAT SOMEHOW A MISTAKE

That was it. I had left the remaining thoughts to drift through the air, not settling anywhere.

I closed my eyes, bringing the letter back to my face, letting the fragrant paper form a small tent across my eyes and nose.

Chapter 2

Markie leaned back in her chair and propped her legs up on the executive desk directly in front of her. She liked this office — the modern furniture that she herself had chosen, the smart knickknacks that hinted at an expensive appreciation of the arts, rare lithographs from a trendy artist from the East Coast, the large window with a view of the city.

She took a moment to survey the rooftops of the smaller buildings, then gazed up and beyond them to the place where the tangerine sky seemed to melt into the Pacific Ocean. Another long day at the office was quietly drawing to a close. It had been rather hectic, but during the last hour, the pace had suddenly slowed. A perfect way to end the day.

A sigh escaped Markie's lips. She glanced at her telephone. She hated the fact that it was so difficult to sit still for more than a few moments when things finally settled down at work. There was something about staying busy that comforted, even reassured her. As soon as things calmed down long enough for her to have time with herself she began to feel edgy, vaguely uncomfortable.

Her eyes fixed on the telephone. That damn telephone seemed to have a deliberateness about it. Markie supposed her borderline resentment toward that simple nuisance was really her own neurosis. Her friends never alluded to their telephones with any animosity, but for Markie, it represented some symbolic internal struggle. As if that piece of electronic equipment could really be taunting her. It was absurd, there was no doubt, and yet Markie had a sudden urge to kick the damn thing off her desk.

It seemed to be staring at her, as though mouthing imaginary words: "That's right, no one has called you today. Oh sure, those business calls come through, but there's no one else, is there, Markie? Looks like you're going to be all alone tonight. All alone."

Markie moved her leg across the desk and accidentally (or so it would appear to the maintenance people who would replace it) knocked the phone over the side of the desk.

As it bounced against the plush carpet, it made a delightful sound, almost as if it were attempting to ring in order to appease her. For a split second,

Markie wondered if that sound was indeed an incoming call and she felt her body jerk in quick response. A call, at last a call! But the ring was short and flat.

Markie leaned over and brought the telephone back to her desk. Without another thought she opened her top desk drawer and pulled out the pocket-sized black address book. Surely there was someone she could call for the evening? She flipped through it, ritualistically turning the pages to review the names of old lovers she had had and then discarded.

There was Julie, eternally available, but did Markie really want to deal with that clinging type tonight? Sandra was always a hot time in bed, but Sandra had been somewhat aggravated with Markie the last time. So maybe Markie had been a little bit selfish, always calling Sandra at the last minute, never quite free when Sandra wanted her to go somewhere. There was Marsha. Markie shook her head as she continued her search through the many uninteresting names that adorned her address book like tiny ornaments on a Christmas tree.

Suddenly the telephone let out a shrill ring. How very clever of it to try to win back Markie's attention. She quickly lifted the receiver.

"Ms. Lewis, there's a woman out here who insists on seeing you. I explained that you're in a meeting, but she refuses to leave until she sees you."

"And *who* is this woman?" Markie replied, irritated that the phone had once again betrayed her, and that somehow her secretary had been a party to this betrayal.

"She won't give her name."

"What? I'm busy, Beverly. Have her leave a number —"

The door flew open and a woman — oh no! it was the woman from the Flowers Bar — came storming into Markie's office. A distraught Beverly followed directly behind her.

"You *will* see me, God damn it!" the woman said.

Markie, stunned that the woman had the nerve to show up at her office and create a potentially nasty scene, turned to Beverly and said, "Yes, of course, that will be all, Beverly."

Beverly looked long and hard at both Markie and the somewhat disheveled intruder, then closed the door. *That* was another thing Markie was going to eventually have to deal with. Hadn't she learned about sleeping with secretaries, especially straight ones?

"How dare you! How dare you!" the woman hissed.

"Please calm down for a moment so we can talk rationally," Markie said coolly, trying to figure out her next move.

Several nights earlier, Markie had had that familiar edgy feeling and hadn't wanted to go home after work. In a last minute decision, she had stopped for a drink and conversation at the Flowers Bar on Market Street. She had noticed a woman, dressed in black, sitting at the other end of the bar. Auburn curls splashed haphazardly around the woman's regal features. Her full lips were painted in a dark berry tint and her skin was honey-gold. Although difficult to ascertain, Markie imagined there were copper-tinted freckles sprinkled across the redhead's aristocratic nose. She had a flair about her, a hypnotic flashiness.

Flash, Markie's impromptu name for the woman, was talking quite seriously to a blonde stocky woman, probably Flash's lover. The two women seemed oblivious to their surroundings, their faces only inches apart. Occasionally, Flash leaned back from her lover to wipe a tear from her eye. Then she'd move in closer, as if she might miss a single breath or sigh if her ear was not close enough to capture it.

Markie watched the woman for perhaps five minutes, intrigued with the intimate dynamics between the two. Flash, teary-eyed, suddenly noticed that Markie was staring at her. As she continued talking into her lover's ear, she held Markie's gaze for a moment, long enough for Markie to feel the bold directness of it. Then, abruptly, Flash turned her eyes away.

Although Markie wasn't really the type for the bar pick up scene, there was something demanding about this woman. Markie couldn't stop staring. Flash didn't connect with Markie again, but for the rest of the evening, Markie suspected that Flash desperately wanted to take another look.

Fifteen minutes or so later, Flash's lover rose from the barstool, gave her a light kiss and left the bar. Markie watched her push her way through the crowd and out through the stained glass front doors.

Markie looked back to the abandoned woman who was still sitting, seemingly staring at her own reflection in the mirror behind the bar. Markie continued to watch her for several minutes, wondering if the blonde was going to return. Perhaps she had run out to the car and would hurry back with a bouquet of flowers. A small expensively wrapped gift? Markie tried to distract herself with the pretzel sticks, slowly twirling them in the bottom of the bowl, unable to keep from looking at mesmerizing Flash.

When the blonde did not return, Markie, in an impulsive move, told the bartender she'd like to buy the woman in black at the end of the bar a drink.

As the bartender presented the message, she motioned toward Markie with a smile.

Not only did the woman shake her head in unmistakable refusal, but she also delivered such an angry look to Markie that Markie was taken aback. In Markie's quick assessment of the situation, this appeared to be more of a dare than a simple "No, thank you."

Markie absolutely could not resist this delicious challenge. Such a feminine woman, such a fiery attitude, Markie thought hungrily, returning the woman's rejection with a hot smile, lifting her drink in a toast of sorts.

Flash turned away, ran her fingers through her long auburn hair, and quickly slid off the bar stool. She took several steps toward the restroom, then slowed her pace barely long enough to toss a last look over her shoulder at Markie, who was still watching her. The woman's irritated expression had a covert smile to it, like a seductive cryptogram. "Can you read me? Can you read me?" it seemed to taunt.

Damn right I can read you, Markie mused, sliding off her own stool and heading toward the bathroom. The woman in black had already disappeared behind the stenciled wooden door to the restrooms. Oh yes! Markie thought in anticipation as she entered the bright yellow, tiled bathroom.

The small sink area was empty. In fact, the whole

bathroom was deserted except for the woman who was not locked in a stall.

Markie turned and bolted the restroom door. Privacy, that's the key to a situation like this, Markie thought, feeling a hot pulling sensation from deep between her legs. The muffled sound of dance music came from out in the bar, but otherwise the room was quiet. Markie could hear the heightened sound of her own breathing.

Why wasn't the woman making any noise? Markie wondered. Everyone rustles or clears her throat or pulls paper. Markie bent to look under the closed stall door. "You all right?" she asked seductively as she tapped on the door. There was no answer.

Markie knocked again. "Open the door," she whispered.

The door opened slowly. The woman peeked through the slit. "What do you want?" she asked, a mixture of hesitancy and annoyance in her voice.

"Oh come on," Markie responded in a sultry tone, pushing the stall door further open as she spoke. "Tell me you don't know what I want. Tell me that you don't want it too."

Markie was an expert in the art of seduction. Some people were natural piano players — from age three they could sit at a piano and play Bach concertos. Others were able to pick up a baseball bat at age five and hit every pitch. Markie, as far back as she could remember, had been a natural in the art of seduction. She had an uncanny ability to read people, to manipulate a situation so that even the most resistant, like this flower whose lover had left only moments before, ended up wanting to sleep with her.

How intimate the two women had seemed in the bar. How touching the tears, the whispering in the ear.

But Markie had known, in that split second the woman's eyes had connected with hers, what lay ahead. She had sensed it even before this buttercup realized it! The sweetness of pursuit!

Markie pushed the door open enough to pry herself into the tiny stall with the woman. "You want me don't you? I knew you needed a hot woman. Let me give you what you need. C'mon, let me give the little lady just what she needs."

The woman, without a word, took a step back, allowing Markie to enter. "Yes," she murmured under her breath, perhaps thinking of her lover who had left, who had hurried off to meet a friend. Perhaps it angered her.

Markie grabbed the woman into her arms, pushing her against the wall, kissing her as she did so. There was a distinct taste of sticky nectar on her lips. Peach?

She slowed her pace, taking time to run her tongue slowly over the sugared borders of the woman's lips.

In response, the woman opened her mouth, allowing her tongue to slowly glide its way to meet the hot rough texture of Markie's tongue.

"Oh yes, so very sweet!" Markie panted as she let her hands slide down and across the woman's firm breasts snugly cradled in her black angora sweater.

"Diamonds in the coal?" Markie remarked as she raised the sweater in hopes of kissing what felt like the most perfect of breasts. She was not disappointed. For under that black sweater, not even cupped in a brassiere, were the most perfect pink breasts that Markie had ever seen.

Without hesitation, Markie fingered the hardened cherry-red nipples. They were, perhaps, one half inch long. In full blossom, they seemed to darken as Markie squeezed their tips.

Markie gently cupped both of them at once. She continued lapping the woman's fruit-flavored mouth as if to suck every last drop of liqueur from her.

Still holding the breasts, Markie slid her hands to the smooth indentation of the waist and then even further down to the surprisingly curved hips that jutted out into a high bubble-like ass.

Markie reached the very place where the uplifted soft buttocks flowed to her thighs. Fortunately, the woman had chosen to wear a skirt on this evening of indiscretion. Markie easily slipped her hands down and around the teasing ass and up under the short black skirt.

No resistance at all. The woman, as Markie expected, slowly allowed her legs to inch apart. Not wanting to seem too available, Markie supposed. Some women had that way of spreading their legs gradually, as if there were some sort of decision to be made, as if they thought, "You've got to make me hot enough. You've got to make me appear to be so out of control that I'll open them like I really want to."

What excited Markie were the moments before a woman was really ready to give in to her arousal, her sexuality, those seconds before it was finally okay to *want* to get fucked, when she could give in to abandon.

Markie picked up the woman and carried her out

to the small sink. Sitting her directly on the edge of its shallow bowl, Markie fell to her knees.

The woman was almost to that place of abandon. The visible pleasure Markie would show when she exposed this woman's pussy, when she forced her hands and face up between those luscious thighs, then, Markie was sure, the woman would spread her legs fully, once and for all.

Markie lifted the skirt and pressed her face against the woman's thighs. A sudden heat radiated from the pink lace panties that surrounded the lips of the woman's pussy.

And the fragrance! Markie, intoxicated by the scent of Chanel, pushed to the center where the burgeoning little pouch of those panties showed an oval-shaped damp spot. The area was soaked, stained with the anticipation of sex. The sight of the woman's desire was even more irresistible to Markie — a connoisseur of the most exotic of tastes — than the peach liqueur that had iced the woman's mouth.

Markie pulled the thin wet panties aside and plunged in with her searching tongue.

The woman had long passed the point of coyness. Her legs were spread as far apart as they would go. She leaned back and wrapped them around Markie's shoulders.

She began to buck, lunging forward to fuck Markie's thick, rough, hardened tongue. Arching, grabbing Markie's hair, she muttered in a deep guttural voice — words about only God knew what — things a woman would say only when she was beginning to come. "Right to it, baby, you know that's how, only there, only there."

And at that very moment, that moment when

climax begins and reality ends, the most disastrous event occurred. The bathroom door, with its faulty lock the manager hadn't seen the need to fix, opened. And there stood the lover!

She had gone to meet a friend for dinner, attempting to assert her need for autonomy in her relationship with her partner. She had only driven a few miles, Markie learned later, when her guilt had overridden her and she had turned the car around . . . stopping only for a moment at "Love's Arose," the florist on the corner of Market.

The bartender — the one with that goddamned secret smile — had said she had seen the woman in black head toward the bathroom.

Overwhelmed first with shock and then an unbearable anger, the lover flung the bouquet of flowers across the small bathroom. The flowers separated in midair, creating a hurricane of blossoms around the room.

"And you! And you!" she screamed, not really directing her fury at either of the two perpetrators in particular.

Other women were heading toward the restroom, surrounding the door trying to peer in at the commotion.

Markie had pulled her drenched face from between the woman's legs. "This all looks most incriminating," she said, "but I can assure you there is a misunderstanding of the largest magnitude." She was wiping her face, trying to move past the lover blocking the door.

From behind the lover, who raised her fists and might have started throwing punches, a large woman pinned the lover's arms, holding her down.

"I think you better get the hell out of here right now," the bouncer said, looking directly at Markie, trying to restrain the lover as best she could.

"Who the hell are you? Who the hell do you think you are!" the lover screamed at Markie, struggling to break away from her captor's tight grip.

Markie, thinking that yes, this would indeed be the best time to leave the bar, made a quick exit past the lover, through the crowd of women and out the large glass doors.

"I swear I'll find you!" the lover was still yelling as the doors closed behind Markie.

Markie looked up at the woman standing before her and motioned to a chair. "Please," she said calmly. "We don't have to create a disturbing scene, do we? I'm most willing to spend as much time as you need. I had no idea that it was *you* when my secretary called. As a matter of fact, it's nice to see you. I didn't get your name —"

"Didn't get my name!" the woman gasped. "Is that what I'm supposed to believe! It's not so difficult to find out who women are in this community. And let me tell you, I've pretty much saved you from getting your ass kicked! My lover is the one who found out who you were. Believe me, she had your name, where you worked, everything, by the end of that night."

"So, am I supposed to be scared that your big,

bad girlfriend is going to get me? Did she send you over as some sort of messenger? C'mon, how the hell was I supposed to know that you two had a steady thing? I mean, *you* never said a word, and in my opinion, you were pretty available for a fuck, considering you and your lover were so tight!"

"Well, we're not tight any more! And no one *fucks* me. Do you understand? I have sex. I *don't* fuck."

"Excuse me," Markie replied, amused by the vituperative princess sitting across from her. Markie was beginning to better understand the situation. This woman wasn't here to start a hassle, nor was she a messenger from the girlfriend. No, this woman was here because she wanted to see Markie again! She was angry because Markie hadn't attempted to track her down.

Markie took a moment to evaluate the woman more carefully. She was indeed striking with her auburn hair tossed around her face in a whirlwind of curls. Her dark brown eyes richly contrasted with her creamy complexion. She wore a black oversized sweater, a long skirt, low boots and thick socks.

"So, then," Markie teased. "You don't fuck. Hmmmm. Do you eat, by any chance? Because, if you do, I know a wonderful restaurant I'd love to take you to."

"Yes," the woman answered, pouting coquettishly. "I *do* eat."

Chapter 3

Ruby opened her eyes and with a quick breath of air she blew the weightless sheet of stationery from her face. It floated briefly, then landed on top of the "back-to-the-closet pile." She brought her hands to her heart, as if she could somehow stop the insistent piercing from within. There was an empty desperation that gnawed deep inside her. Life had seemed simple before she walked out on Lenny. Before she had somehow, as if in a clouded trance, ended up at Markie's office. How many months had passed? Ruby felt an unexpected disorientation.

In the Flowers Bar, she had been caught totally off guard by that woman's deliberate stare! Those eyes had penetrated her very soul! She had tried to turn away. To this day she remembered the intentional closing of her eyes, the intentional refusal to respond, wanting to believe that she absolutely would not cheat on Lenny again. And yet, something had gotten out of control, twisted. And before she had a chance to — what? to say no? to leave the bar? — she had found herself in the restroom, perched up on that cool sink.

And then there was Lenny. Lenny, who had unexpectedly walked in . . . Lenny, who had afterwards wanted to work things out, who had had so little sense of herself that she was somehow able to deny what she had witnessed — Ruby, with legs spread, wrapped around Markie, leaning back, launching into orgasm.

As if there could possibly have been a chance for them! As if Ruby could have ever stayed in a relationship with someone as spineless, as hopeless, as Lenny had been later that evening at her apartment. At first quite impressive, Lenny's initial rush of anger had ricocheted around the small walls of the restroom. Where had that passion disappeared to? At what point had Lenny's self-confident intensity evaporated into pleading and begging?

Ruby had sat on Lenny's couch, and tried to reassure Lenny that things were workable, but in her heart she was aware of a sickening urge to rush into Lenny's bathroom and vomit.

It would never be the same. Ruby had leaned over the toilet for what felt like an hour. She could hear Lenny moving around the apartment, humming, as if things had been settled, as if things would be normal again.

It had been like it always was for Ruby. She had believed that with Lenny she had found a lover exciting enough to hold her complete interest. Finally, she would be content in a relationship. And how long had she been fulfilled with Lenny? This had not been the first fling she had had since she and Lenny had gotten together, but it was by and large the most damaging. Lenny had sat in the living room, her face in her hands, and said it would be different in the future. They would both make changes. Ruby had felt heated, dizzy, nauseated. Ruby had known, from the very second Lenny had walked into the restroom, flowers swirling in all directions, even as the bouncer had tried to contain Lenny, that things would go no further. Lenny would somehow try to forget the whole sordid affair, and she, herself, would begin to obsess unmercifully about the incredible woman in the bar who had played her so well. Knowing that if it was the last thing she ever did, she would find that woman, she would have her again.

Chapter 4

As I sit here going over some of my past experiences, I wonder what the point is. After all, I've learned what I've needed to learn. I no longer play any of the old games. But thinking back, there were some times, some pretty hot times.

Isn't that just like me, so ready to forget the way it *really* was — saying that it was hot! That's exactly how I used to end up in trouble. There were adventures before Markie, but I had no conception of how out of control I had become. My life story? Hard drama, erotic struggle, a beauty on the outside, dominated by the beast within.

I've enjoyed my life, but up until Markie, I *was* somewhat self-centered. I did things for my own satisfaction, regardless of who I used or who got hurt. Anyone and anything was fair game as long as I got what I needed. I suppose I did have a bit of a reputation as a femme fatale.

No matter what I did, women were crazy for me. They were always ready to take a chance, even if it was a best friend who was currently crying over me. And I never seemed to have to pay the consequences for any of my actions — at least not at that time. Markie took care of the pay-back in one big karmic avalanche. But that came later.

When my current lover, Susan, and I first got together, I would think of Markie whenever things got difficult between us. Should I give Markie a chance? Should I contact her? It had been good. Things might get better. It was as if little demons were whispering in my ear, tempting me to call Markie, though I knew full well that that sort of behavior would ultimately pull me away from Susan. The old pattern — start an affair when a relationship gets too intimate — was decorated in a flashy new package: "Go back to Markie."

I did not want to threaten my relationship with Susan, and contact with Markie fell into that category. Consequently, I made an adamant decision not to see, or even think about, Markie.

The letter I had written to Markie was like a

Pandora's box. After all these months, what harm would there be in opening it, just peeking in?

But after I read the letter, I had an unexpected compulsion to review every last intense detail. So I figured I would permit myself to think about Markie under one condition: no obsessing about her. I wanted to look at my part in the matter — who I was before Markie, how it *really* was with Markie — sort of a psychological survey. I would not dwell on romantic illusions of what might have been nor how Markie might be feeling now. Nothing that could cause problems with Susan.

To begin in the beginning, Valerie was my lover Cathy's best friend from college. Cathy and I had been together for about six months when Valerie moved back to town from Las Vegas. She had worked as a showgirl in one of the big casinos until she was offered a modeling job here. She was taller than I am, and as femme, though femme women usually don't even tempt me. But Valerie had a persuasive sexuality about her, one that I couldn't seem to avoid.

She was wealthy. No, not from her job. She had inherited a trust fund when she turned twenty-five. She was discreet about it because she was afraid that people would be interested in her only for her money. But within two weeks of her re-entering the lesbian community here in Northern California, everyone else knew about it.

Valerie started seeing Cathy quite a bit and consequently we were frequently thrown together. Cathy worked a revolving schedule, alternating day and night shifts, so there were many evenings when it was just Valerie and me.

One night, after Cathy had left for work, we were sitting in Cathy's apartment watching a video about New York City. Knowing we were going to stay in, I wore my most comfortable pair of jeans and an oversized T-shirt. My curls were tied back with a ribbon, tucked under an old Stetson hat. Valerie had braided her full blonde hair, although the shorter strands fell loosely about her perfect face. She was wearing thick, black, librarian-like glasses as though purposely trying to contrast her striking beauty. I have to admit, on Valerie, the look was sexy.

I had kept my sexual feelings for Valerie pretty much in check. After all, I didn't want to hurt Cathy, and Valerie *was* Cathy's best friend. But that night, watching the New York movie, things took an irreversible turn.

Valerie was eating popcorn and accidentally kicked the whole bowl off the couch. When we both moved quickly in an attempt to stop the mishap, we hit heads. Hard.

We smashed with such an intensity that I was momentarily stunned. As I closed my eyes I saw a flash of blinding light, and then there was complete blackness. It took a second or two for me to reorient myself. After that I felt fine.

But Valerie was on the floor, her eyes shut. I guess I panicked. I threw myself on top of Valerie and put my mouth on hers.

I can't tell you how surprised I was when she opened her eyes and whispered, "Oh, yes!"

We were surrounded by popcorn. The song, "New York, New York," played cheerfully in the background. And Valerie, beautiful Valerie, was pressed beneath me. Oh yes.

I placed my cheek against hers and was swept into a sweet blend of Shalimar and blonde hair. Her body was deliciously soft and I could feel her breasts rise and fall with each breath she took.

I lifted myself partially up from Valerie and stared at her smooth, porcelain-like face. "You okay?" I asked, only too aware of the feel of her plush curved body that yielded so gracefully under mine.

"Yes," Valerie whispered, taking a long moment to appraise me carefully, to grasp me with her demanding eyes. "I'm *very* okay."

I looked down at her, popcorn framing her sun-blonde hair, her black glasses crooked on her face, and said with a giggle, "Why are we whispering?"

Suddenly, we were both laughing. What a sight we must have been, smashed together in a bed of popcorn!

I was balanced on my elbows which were beginning to ache. My choice was either to lie back on top of her or get up. I glanced over toward the TV, the skyline of New York at night was glittering like a jewel-laden bracelet. This was my lover's best friend who felt so good under my aroused body. *Someone* in this situation had to exercise self-control.

"Some city, huh," I said, pulling myself up off this enticing woman. Perhaps this was all a mistake. Perhaps Valerie was merely telling me she wasn't hurt, that I was reading more into the situation than was warranted. Even in a relationship as solid as Cathy's and mine, I was already imagining reasons for an affair. No. Not this time!

Valerie propped herself up, reaching for my arm

in the same movement. "I'll take you there tonight, to New York, on the town. We could be on a plane within the next hour or two, on our way to New York . . ."

Now what was that supposed to mean? I turned toward her, just as she leaned up to place her full pink lips on mine. I felt a rush of warmth pass between our lips as she hesitated flirtatiously, only millimeters away. An intense quiver passed through me and I heard the sound of her mouth opening, a slight clicking noise as her lips parted. Her tongue frosted her dry lips with sweet, dew-like saliva, and then she pressed that hot moist mouth against mine.

She brought her hand to the back of my head, pulling me to her. I couldn't move as she drew my tongue into her mouth.

Moaning, she ran her tongue around the inside of my mouth. I felt a sudden lack of control as I grabbed her head with my own hand, as if God forbid, she would try to pull away.

"You don't know how much I've wanted this!" I heard my own voice murmuring in between the luscious kisses.

"I thought so. I could just feel the electricity between us like I've never felt before!"

Sure. Like she "never felt before." And same for me, right? First time for both of us.

"Me neither," I sighed.

"I mean it!" Valerie exclaimed, pulling away from me. "We could leave for New York right now! It's the weekend. We can tell Cathy we went shopping. She's working graveyard anyway. C'mon, you and me. Let me take you to breakfast in Greenwich Village."

Just like that, I thought. Jump on a plane with good ol' nobody-knows-is-wealthy Val. Fly across the country to New York City for breakfast.

I wasn't looking to cheat on Cathy, but as my Mom used to say, "Sweetheart, don't ruin your life by missing out on life's opportunities when they come knocking on your door."

I thought back to the family legend about Grandmother Tessie. She used to sit in her rocking chair the last few years of her life, just rocking and staring, shaking her head and repeating the now famous family phrase: "I let my *whole* life pass me by, sacrificed everything for Sidney, for what? For him to run off with a tramp!"

No. I wouldn't do this for the selfish purpose of having an affair. I would go to New York with Valerie for the sake of Grandmother Tessie.

"Yes!" I said hotly, my hungry mouth back on Valerie's sizzling lips. "I need to call Cathy and tell her that —"

I took a long moment to think. If I said I was going on a weekend trip with Val, Cathy would protest. I needed an excuse that was completely innocuous. Within seconds, I was on the phone with Cathy, letting her know that I had changed my mind and was going to attend the Conference on Women's History down in San Luis Obispo after all.

"What conference?" she responded, rather confused.

"You know — I sit and tell you things, and I swear you're not paying attention to me. This is a perfect example! Don't you remember the conversation we had about —"

"I do too listen!" Cathy interrupted. "Perhaps if you spent a little more time on each subject rather than jumping around like you do when you talk, I'd remember more."

"Are we having a fight?" I replied, allowing a hint of concern to discreetly shadow my words. "Because if you are upset with me about something, there's no way I'm going anywhere! You are the primary thing in my life! You know that, don't you?" I looked at Valerie who was blowing a kiss to me from across the room.

"You are *such* a sweetheart to put up with me, sometimes," Cathy said, her voice softer now. "You're right, I guess I don't listen to everything you say, and I'm premenstrual. I want you to go and have a good time. There's a fifty-dollar bill in the desk drawer, in the green envelope. Take it with you and buy yourself something pretty from me."

"Oh, Cathy, I couldn't . . ."

"Not another word. Call me when you get back, okay?"

"Okay," I answered, blowing a kiss into the phone. New York City here I come! I thought with a rush of anticipation as I returned the receiver to the telephone.

"Ready?" Valerie said with a smile, sensing my excitement.

"I need to stop by my place and get my clothes and I'll be set," I answered.

"Oh, you don't seem to understand," Valerie said coolly. "*I'll* be buying you everything you're going to need in New York."

Valerie turned to the coat rack to get our jackets.

Meanwhile, I reached into the desk drawer, pulled out the envelope and stuffed the fifty-dollar bill into my pants pocket. Grandma Tessie, I thought, this one's for you!

Chapter 5

"I think you need that bracelet," Valerie whispered in my ear as we leaned over the counter in the San Francisco Airport gift shop. "It goes perfectly with your ring."

"Flight six two two for New York now boarding at gate twenty-seven."

"Isn't that our flight?" I asked, thinking that Valerie had not heard the announcement.

"Don't worry, we have time," she said matter-of-factly as she continued to look at the thick gold bracelet in the display case.

"Excuse me, miss," Valerie was saying, motioning for the sales clerk. "We want that bracelet, right there."

She was pointing, not bothering to worry if it would fit . . . of course it would fit. Gold *always* fits. She handed over her charge card and wrapped her arms around me, unconcerned that a woman with a tight bun was staring at us from across the gift shop, seemingly displeased with our obviously lesbian relationship.

Valerie gave me a slight nudge, drawing my attention away from the woman and back to the bracelet. "Put out your wrist," she said as she lifted the bracelet out of the red Cartier box. "I want to see you in gold."

I had to admit, the bracelet was extraordinary.

She fastened the clasp. "You're the kind of woman who deserves gifts," she said with a smile. "*I* know how to appreciate a woman like you."

Deserves gifts? What an interesting concept. And the more I thought about that premise, the more I liked it.

"Yes," I said simply.

I glanced around the gift shop for the woman with the bun, but she had left. I leaned forward and gave Valerie a light kiss on the lips. "Thank you," I said. "It's a most beautiful gift."

"Final call for Flight six two two to New York now boarding at gate . . ."

"That's us!" Valerie said excitedly. She grabbed my hand and began pulling me behind her.

She raced down the corridor, dragging me along, past the long span of gates until we finally reached gate twenty-seven. Everyone else had already boarded the plane. We hurried toward the flight attendant who reached for our boarding passes as we flew by her.

Valerie was laughing. "I love the risk!"

The risk? I thought. Of missing the plane?

We moved into the cabin. I couldn't help but notice the woman with the bun sitting directly behind my seat with a stern expression on her face. She gave me a nasty look, as if it were my fault the plane had not departed yet — as if somehow, in my own lesbian way, I had inconvenienced her.

"She's an old bag, don't let her get to you," Valerie hissed into my ear as if she read my thoughts. "Trust me, I'll have your mind off her in minutes."

We sat down. The crew prepared for departure. I let out a long breath, feeling the plane vibrate as it ascended. The lights from the city sparkled and folded into the black velvet sky.

First-class seats, of course were one of the advantages of traveling with a lover who was wealthy. I looked down at the bracelet that adorned my arm. Another advantage. I closed my eyes, swallowing a sip of the champagne that Valerie had ordered for us. What was it, eleven-thirty p.m.? Sitting on an airplane, flying to New York — to have breakfast in the morning? This was the life! A life I could get used to. A life that I deserved. With my looks, my brains, I *deserved* to be treated in a special way, and it took a woman like Valerie to help me to realize that elementary fact.

I took another sip from the glass, feeling the

warmth of the alcohol move through my body. I've never been a big drinker, so it didn't take much for me to feel the effects of the champagne.

Valerie was whispering in my ear about how hot she thought I was, how she'd never met a woman like me, how she wanted to win me away from Cathy even at the expense of their friendship. She refilled my glass as she spoke, smiling, taking it all in.

Valerie pulled a blanket over our laps. How comfortable and roomy first-class seats were! The plane was dark except for the overhead lights that the passengers, the few that had chosen to stay awake, were quietly reading their books under. The blanket was thrown loosely over my legs. The alcohol pulsated quickly through my body with each beat of my heart.

"I want to have you, right here on the plane," Valerie murmured in my ear as she moved her hand under the blanket and began unfastening my pants.

My head was swirling. I felt good. Very good indeed. She wanted to have me, right here, first class. I had had my share of adventurous sex . . . but on an airplane? God only knew how many miles up we were, racing across the sky in a silver bullet, surrounded by an odd assortment of midnight travelers, including the lady with the bun. I shifted my head slightly, trying to get a better idea of who was actually awake. The plane was dark, quiet. Who would know? Valerie's cool fingers moved down onto the smooth skin of my stomach, trying to sneak their way deeper and deeper toward my thick nest of hair.

"Pull them down. Pull your pants down right now."

That's what I liked about Valerie — she knew

exactly what she wanted and went for it without a second thought, like taking me to New York just because she wanted to, best friend be damned. Like buying the gold bracelet, even though our flight had been announced and even threatened to leave without us. She wanted the bracelet, she got it. And now, just from the very tone in her voice, I knew there really wasn't a question as to whether I'd take down my pants for her. She wanted it, and that was that.

I pulled my pants down around my knees.

"No. All the way off," Valerie said panting in my ear.

Hmm. All the way off. I managed to slip my legs out of the pants leaving them in a discreet little pile under my feet, hoping that I had dropped them in such a way that they'd slip back on easily — just in case that sort of fast action were to become necessary. I took a deep breath.

Valerie took a sip from her glass, leaned over close to me, and placed her champagne-coated lips on mine. I opened my mouth (no sense playing it coy at this point) to give her what I planned to be quite a kiss. But instead, Valerie opened her lips to dribble a warmed mouthful of champagne down my chin, my neck, and down my blouse.

"Oh!" she said in mock alarm. "So very, very sorry!" She ripped my blouse open. The top three buttons flew off and over the side of my blanketed legs. "Let me get this before it has a chance to stain!"

She was licking, rapidly moving her tongue down my neck, across my chest. She lapped, quickly sucking at my champagne-flavored breasts.

I like a good time, but I did have a brief vision of

the lights going on, the flight attendant passing by, the lady with the bun standing up and peeking over the seat.

Valerie had taken another swallow of champagne, and must have filled her mouth completely, because when she kissed me this time, a waterfall of liquid began cascading down my face and breasts, into my lap.

I was soaked, my torn blouse was drenched, the lushly upholstered first-class seat was dampened, and Valerie seemed out of control.

"Your breasts are absolutely beautiful!" Valerie gushed. "I just *had* to have you, darling."

I was trying to bring the blanket up further to screen my exposed breasts. And yet there was something extraordinarily exciting about the whole thing — champagne everywhere, the flight attendant only a few rows away. I glanced down as Valerie slowly pulled her lips away from my extended nipples. I ached for more.

I felt myself unexpectedly arch, attempting to entice Valerie to latch back onto my throbbing nipples. Without hesitation, Valerie took the bait and began sucking — first one, then, bringing my breasts together with her hands, both my nipples simultaneously.

I let go of the blanket and cupped my breasts together for her, desperately wanting her to dip her fingers down into my champagne-marinated pussy.

She was still tugging, coaxing my nipples to harden even more, as if that was possible! Finally, her hands slid down to my waist and then continued to the very center of my sexual heat.

"Spread your legs for me, Ruby."

Valerie had let go of my pellet-like nipples, worked her way down between the seats and placed herself directly between my legs, pulling the blanket partially over her head to create a tent over my legs and her body.

Without a moment's delay, she moved closer. I could feel the heat from her mouth perhaps an inch from my pounding clit. I wanted to slam my pussy up against her face! But I was immobilized, almost pinned, now that Valerie had moved in between my legs.

Lightly, unbearably softly, her tongue grazed against the tightened skin of my erect clitoris. Teasing, she hardly connected with the tissues at all, but just enough so that I could feel the tip of her tongue flicking ever so slightly on the tiny tipped pink nugget.

"Please!" I whispered, out of control with passion. "Lick it, press it hard with your tongue."

"Oh, sweetheart," Valerie responded, a self-satisfied tone to her voice. "I don't think I can do that just yet. Please, if you would be a dear, ring for another glass of champagne?"

Ring for the attendant! And what was Valerie going to do while I ordered her drink?

As if she could read my thoughts, Valerie said seductively, "No sense in either of us getting uncomfortable. I'll just stay under the blanket here. The attendant will never notice."

Under normal circumstances, I would have never conceded to such a suggestion, but at that point I was so aroused, so worked up, that I would have done anything to get Valerie's hot tongue back onto my pussy. I pushed the call button.

The flight attendant, only three rows away, was next to me in seconds.

"Yes?" she said quietly, not wanting to disturb the other sleeping travelers.

Valerie, under the blanket, took the voice as a cue to resume licking. Gently, she began to slide that warm tongue of hers between my full lips. The sensation was so delicate that it took me a moment to realize exactly what she was doing.

"I'd like some more champagne please," I said, trying to keep my voice steady, natural-sounding.

"Another bottle, same as the first?" The attendant studied my face carefully.

Valerie continued to lightly tap her tongue against my hard, thick wedge of skin.

"Yes, that would be perfect," I answered, my voice suddenly cracking.

As the attendant walked toward the bar, Valerie began to whip her tongue against my clitoris, creating a lashing sensation.

"Valerie, please, she'll be back any second. Surely you don't want her to . . ."

Valerie responded by pulling my legs further apart, diving even deeper between my fleshy lips, sinking her tongue into my wet slit.

"Oh God," I murmured. I leaned my head back into my seat, brushing up against the attendant who was now standing directly above me with an opened champagne bottle in her hand.

"Excuse me?" she said, her voice casual. Or did I hear a slight but distinct edge to it? Did she wonder where my traveling companion had disappeared to? Or did she know *exactly* where Valerie was? Was the crew standing in the back, watching with alarmed interest at the spectacle we were making?

"Yes, the champagne, thank you."

Valerie's fingers were stretching the lips of my pussy far apart to allow her better access. She rubbed her entire face up and down the slick flesh so that I could smell the light, musky fragrance beginning to permeate the blanket. She nibbled, flicked, then sucked the erect tissues. I was doing everything I could to keep from arching up, from crying out in pleasure.

The attendant handed the medium-sized bottle to me. "Can I get you anything else?" she said with a thin smile, as if she could also smell my scent.

Valerie pumped her tongue roughly in and out of my vagina. The blanket rising and falling with each thrust. I was beside myself. The tension was becoming too much. The attendant was still staring as an incredibly wild Valerie tongue-fucked me so hard I could not speak. Could I, would I, orgasm in front of the attendant? I kept a smile glued to my face, tried not to yell the phrase that was beginning to push its way out of my mouth into the quiet cabin of the airplane, that simple desperate plea, "Fuck me hard."

"Is there anything else?" she repeated, looking at me with a perplexed expression.

"I . . . I . . ." I was stumbling into orgasm, a ridiculous grin plastered on my face. Valerie's tongue stabbed into me over and over, stopping only momentarily to move up and over my engorged shaft, then returning to my pulsating opening.

I put my hands under the blanket, quite out of myself, grabbing onto Valerie's hair. My body seemed to be shuddering with pleasure.

Was the attendant merely waiting for a reply or was she frozen, not believing the sight she was witnessing?

"Yes . . . yes . . . no . . ." I muttered as I rode out the orgasm. And then, trying to sound casual, even matter-of-fact, I murmured, "I'm fine, thank you."

The stewardess glanced down to the blanket that had suddenly stopped moving, then back to me.

"Enjoy the champagne." She turned and walked away.

Valerie lifted the blanket. Immediately the sex fragrance surrounded me in a small wave of heat. She poked her head out and said with a grin, "I see *you* also take pleasure in risk!"

I leaned my head back with a sigh.

Chapter 6

The fact that Ruby had made the sudden decision to leave Lenny and start up an affair with Markie was not that unpredictable. Ruby had always had a driving force within her. She was constantly searching for "The One," a fantasy person who would fill her up, keep her from wanting to have affairs. Every time she broke a commitment, or "became a party to an indiscretion," as she was often overheard saying to a close friend, she would eventually end up leaving her current partner to be with the new adventure, the newer lover.

Ruby was sincere when she'd look into her partner's eyes and make a long-term commitment, but somehow or other, Ruby eventually would find herself in the arms of someone new. Ruby saw herself as a victim of circumstances.

The incident with Valerie was typical. How very bold of Ruby to fly across the country with Cathy's best friend! Had she no sense of values, no ethics? She even took Cathy's fifty-dollar bill and stuffed it in her pocket before departing!

And yet, Ruby had an answer for everything. The fifty dollars? Ruby found a beautiful music box for Cathy in an antique store in Greenwich Village. It was a gift Cathy adored. but that attractive knickknack that, ironically, played "I Love You Truly" each time the porcelain lid was raised, didn't do much to ease the pain. The following weekend, Ruby announced that somehow, Valerie and she had, as Ruby had explained to a dismayed Cathy, "started this thing."

And then there was Lenny, who still carries a bitterness in her heart that even her closest friends dare not allude to. She hasn't been in a relationship since Ruby, and swears that she has no intentions of being in one. Not ever.

That fateful evening in Markie's office, Ruby swirled in obsessive fury, only to be wooed into dining at one of the most exclusive restaurants in San Francisco. There was no turning back for her.

One thing is certain when it comes to Ruby: give her adventure, spend money on her, and she becomes a most exciting companion.

Valerie treated Ruby as though she were of royal blood. The pampering! The over-indulging! The constant gifts! Ruby had always demanded special treatment from her lovers in the past. She even admitted to having "a *small* seedling of selfishness buried somewhere deep inside," but the relationship with Valerie progressed as if that tender little seed were blanketed in supersoil and spoon-fed with sunlight until it blossomed into a monstrous plant.

Not until Valerie had Ruby been so money-oriented, so deserving, as it were. Their relationship lasted only a few months, until Valerie had to go back to Las Vegas for some contest for "Showgirl of the Year." Ruby refused to go. She was *already* getting a bit tired of Valerie's monotonous jealousies. After all, the affair with Lenny didn't really start until Valerie was well on her way to Las Vegas.

In that short time with Valerie, Ruby experienced a kind of metamorphosis, emerging from her cocoon believing herself to be a princess, and anyone interested in her company, who wanted to win her into bed, had to shower her with gifts and attention and to basically spoil her rotten.

Lenny, who followed Valerie in Ruby's string of affairs, also spoiled Ruby right up to the very end, until Lenny decided against Ruby's wishes to have dinner with a friend.

But Markie was different. On the evening of their first dinner, she and Ruby sat in one of the special booths the exclusive restaurant was known for. The secluded booth had a curtain that pulled closed, leaving the occupants to enjoy their dinner in the utmost privacy. It was a spot frequented quite often by Markie.

The maitre d', upon seeing Markie, discreetly led them to their booth. He offered to bring them a vintage wine, perhaps champagne, knowing full well that Markie would hesitate, as if making a new decision. She requested Dom Perignon, as she always did, as though this was an occasion out of the ordinary, as if this particular woman she was escorting was indeed a prize that deserved something special.

Ruby felt drawn to the attractive woman ordering the expensive champagne for her. She would love some champagne. Dom Perignon was a favorite of hers. How could Markie have guessed!

The teal shirt Markie wore complemented her olive complexion. Her black sport coat was tailored to fit her athletic build perfectly. How sure of herself Markie was! She took over from the start, opening doors for Ruby — something that even Valerie didn't do — walking on the street-side of the sidewalk, as if shielding Ruby from a careening car or flying object from a building's upper window. For that was how that custom first came into being. Markie chose the most luxurious of restaurants and ordered the right champagne. It was like something out of a dream.

Ruby, a moderate drinker, was already tipsy from the champagne before the hors d'oeuvres arrived at the table. Oysters, lightly seasoned and broiled, perched in their petal-like shells, waiting to be plucked. Ruby had a sudden urge to take her index finger and run it gently down the fleshy plump meat of the oyster. How very smooth, how distinctly familiar it felt! She flicked the little tuft of oyster tissue, then brought her warm finger to her mouth, letting the spices awaken her taste buds. Her mouth watered in response to the hint of garlic. Ruby licked the tip of her finger and touched the inflated oyster, which seemed to have swollen. She grazed the side of the succulent meat.

"Oysters are one of my favorite delicacies . . ." Markie said in a low, sultry voice. She watched Ruby closely. Ruby sensed in Markie a combination of amusement and sexual arousal as Ruby ran her fingertip across the thick oyster. It seemed to burgeon from its confining shell.

"I've never had them before," Ruby said, looking at Markie. "But there *is* something appealing about them. Such an unusual look, such an interesting surface . . ."

"Oh, Ruby," Markie said, lifting an oyster and slowly prying the meat off its shell. "Open your mouth and let me show you how the texture feels on your tongue."

Ruby parted her lips enough for Markie to place the fat little oyster on her tongue.

"Here's the secret." Markie took another sip of champagne and added more to Ruby's nearly empty glass. "Don't chew it. Just roll your tongue around it for a minute or two. Yes. That's exactly right."

Ruby slid the oyster back and forth in her mouth, gently sucking on the flap of meat as she did so. A small spurt of juice escaped from her mouth as she flattened the oyster between her tongue and her palate.

Markie quickly reached for her napkin and daubed the splash from Ruby's thick lower lip. "You like that, Ruby?" she said, not bothering to hide the sexual undertone in her voice. She continued to lightly run the napkin across Ruby's mouth.

Ruby, still sucking on the oyster, was completely lost in the sensation of the spongy feel of the flesh sliding across her tongue, the inside of her lips, her cheeks.

Markie let the napkin fall onto the table. She then brought her finger back to Ruby's lips that were greedily clamped closed. "Let me in, Ruby," she murmured as she tried to separate Ruby's lips.

Markie tried to force her finger into the warm, moist cave that housed the slippery puffed meat, but Ruby wasn't ready to give up the oyster just yet. There was something very titillating about gliding it, sucking it.

Markie pushed even harder against the tightened lips. "Let me in," she implored, slightly smiling.

This is very hot, very hot! Ruby thought as Markie opened Ruby's lips just enough to push her thumb and index finger in. Markie latched onto the oyster and slowly, very slowly began to pull it out.

Ruby moaned as she felt the warm oyster dragged across her tightened lips. Markie tugged the little clump of meat perhaps only an eighth of an inch at a time. Ruby tried to suck it back in, to clamp down on it, but Markie unhurriedly drew out the stretched oyster.

Suddenly, Ruby opened her lips slightly, letting a deep sigh escape. And at that very moment, Markie snapped the oyster from Ruby's mouth, causing an ejaculation of saliva to spew from Ruby's reddened lips onto her chin.

"I *like* oysters." Ruby looked Markie directly in the eyes as she lifted her champagne glass to her spicy lips.

"Yes," Markie replied with a provocative smile. "I thought perhaps you would."

Chapter 7

Markie knew she had the uncanny ability to create the perfect atmosphere in order to achieve a goal — true to her style as a "bon amie," a lover extraordinaire. She knew she handled waiters with style and expertise. "Yes, the lady will have this. No, the lady would prefer that . . ." She left handsome tips, insisting that her conquest stay in the entrance of the restaurant until the parking attendant brought the white Mercedes around to the front. When Markie decided she wanted someone — and the entrancing, multifaceted Ruby fit into her requirements — Markie went out of her way to ensure success.

Ruby had caught Markie's attention — first in the Flowers Bar when Ruby had glanced over her shoulder toward Markie, exciting her, only moments after her lover had departed, then when Ruby had opened the bathroom stall door allowing Markie to enter. She had spread her legs up and around Markie with such abandon, propped up on that cool sink — and then as she had burst into Markie's office like a tropical storm. And now, later that evening, Ruby had flirtatiously attempted to tantalize Markie throughout the course of the dinner.

Markie had a title for women who played the community. There weren't that many women who were true experts in the art of working a woman, who chose a challenge and then won her over. It was a real talent. There was Markie for one, an artist supreme! And there was Sybil — a Don Juanette — who in Markie's opinion let her reputation take a serious dive when she fell in love and was subsequently dumped by, of all people, Margot. Alex — very cool, smooth Alex — was another. She had even had the guts to try to seduce Markie! And there was Ramone, "Ms. Macho" from Walnut Creek, a woman Markie alternately despised and respected. Now, added to the list, there was this hot little number Ruby.

Ruby was unusual. Not many femmes played a good game, knew how to work the women, but Markie sensed that Ruby was a member of the elite "Players," as Markie referred to this select group of women. And there was nothing, *absolutely nothing* better for a player's reputation than to work another player, to lure her in, capture her heart, and then unexpectedly break her down.

"You seem to have enjoyed the meal," Markie said as she opened the car door for Ruby. "I like a woman who's not afraid to take pleasure in eating. So many times I've dined with women who barely would touch their food . . ."

Ruby, still slightly intoxicated from the champagne and delicious meal, murmured in agreement as she climbed into the front seat of Markie's plush automobile. A flyaway fantasy floated into Ruby's mind — Markie pulling that moist oyster from between her lips and running it alongside of her thickened clitoral shaft. She felt a trembling deep within her body.

Markie closed the car door and slowly walked over to the driver's side, watching Ruby through the window as she did so. This woman wants me to take her home, wants to be fucked, Markie thought. She unlocked the car door and slid in.

"Ruby," Markie said under her breath, lifting her arm up and around Ruby and pulling her close. Without another word, Markie turned and kissed Ruby directly on the lips. A light, gentle kiss, her lips pressed against Ruby's plush pink mouth as though Ruby were a fragile bird. This kiss demonstrated a sort of specialness — not born out of lust, not a suggestion of sex — but a simple "this is something out of the ordinary" kiss. At least, that was the intention behind Markie's technique.

Ruby moaned slightly. She wasn't quite sure of what it was about Markie that made her feel like she never had felt before. Oh sure, she knew she had had that same feeling at the beginning of many relationships, but this time, something was different.

"I want to go home with you," Ruby said quietly. The mood had shifted and whispering seemed a requisite after a kiss like that.

Markie softly cupped Ruby's face. "When I first met you at the Flowers Bar, I was overwhelmed by your provocativeness. I had to have you. But now, after spending time with you, I want to go slower, get to know you, savor every moment with you." Yes, Markie thought, this woman, broken down, will be quite a trophy.

"Can't we go slowly *together?* We could just hold each other, we don't have to make love." Ruby leaned closer wondering what the hell was going on. Since when did Ruby have to persuade someone to go to bed with her, especially someone she had already had sex with?

Markie kissed her lightly on the cheek. "Trust me, my sweet Ruby. You are something to be cherished. I only want things to be absolutely perfect," Markie whispered gently into Ruby's ear.

She turned to face the steering wheel and then, as though just realizing it, said quickly, "Damn! I think I left my wallet in the booth. I'll be right back."

"Sure." Ruby watched Markie jump out of the car and run up the steps to the restaurant. This was very new for Ruby, the abrupt emptiness she felt as soon as Markie left the car. "I'm in trouble," she whispered aloud, shaking her head. "I don't know exactly how, but I'm definitely in trouble."

* * * * *

Markie entered the restaurant and moved quickly over to the maitre d'.

"A problem, Ms. Lewis?"

"Oh no, Charles. I just need the phone."

"Yes, of course," he answered, lifting the push-button telephone from under the counter.

Markie quickly thumbed through her address book, found Sandra's number and dialed. With a little patience, she would have Ruby all to herself, but for tonight, to tide her over, there was always Sandra — hot, spicy Sandra.

"Yes, Beautiful, it's me . . . how about letting me come hold you the way you need it tonight?" Markie paused. "You know I do . . . give me a half hour . . . got to drop off an assignment I'm working on and I'll be right over."

"Have a good evening, Ms. Lewis," Charles said as Markie gave him a quick wave.

"I certainly will," she said with a smug smile.

Chapter 8

"Ruby, this is Lenny. Can't we try to work something out? Please call me." Beep. "Hi Ruby, it's me, Valerie. Thought maybe you'd like to come for lunch in New Orleans Thursday? Call me if you can figure a way to join me." Beep. "Ruby, this is Jean. I met you at Lenny's office a few weeks ago. She told me about you two breaking up and all. I'm really sorry to hear about it. I was wondering if you're not already busy tonight, perhaps you'd like a friend?" Beep. "Hey, Rube, it's Carmen. Did you go see her? How'd it go? If I know you, lady, I probably won't hear from you for a few days. Not till she brings you home, ha!"

Ruby turned away from the answering machine. She still couldn't figure it out. She had expected Markie to wine, dine, fuck and then fall quite in love with her. Instead, Markie brought her home . . . and rather early at that.

Ruby appraised herself carefully in the full-length mirror. She looked good. Although not beautiful, she had an exotic flair. Her thick auburn curls cascaded loosely around her face, emphasizing her creamy complexion. The sprinkle of freckles across her Grecian nose accentuated the bronze tint in her brown eyes. She had a slender build, yet her body was graced with luscious curves.

She fluffed up her hair and approached the mirror, bringing her lips a breath away from the glass. "Oh, Markie" she whispered, peeking from beneath her nearly closed eyelids, trying to get an idea of how she had looked during that final goodnight kiss. Lightly she pressed her mouth against the cool glass.

"What the hell am I doing!" Ruby said aloud. "Of course I looked okay, I always look okay! If this woman is smart, she'll come after *me.* I don't need to chase after her. I've done my part, now it's up to her. I only ask once!"

Ruby stepped away and took one last look in the mirror. "She'll be begging for it soon enough." Ruby replayed the messages on the answering machine, scribbling Jean's phone number on a memo pad. She glanced at her watch — nine p.m., Friday night . . .

"I don't sit around and wait for anyone!" she said sharply as she dialed Jean's number.

Chapter 9

So I used Jean. Was that such a big deal? Anyway, she's the one who called me, albeit looking to befriend a poor broken heart. I didn't expect her to be home, let alone available at nine o'clock on a Friday night. I needed to distract myself from the unnerving feeling I'd had since Markie had dropped me off. You could say that I was merely looking for some company, and somehow or other I became a victim of circumstances.

I couldn't stand that Markie didn't want to go to bed with me! The negotiator from my intellectual side thought it was exciting to find someone who seemed to want to establish a stronger basis for a relationship. I should feel fortunate that Markie wanted to develop something more meaningful. But another part of me, "Her Highness, The Emotions," was angry. My charisma in bed was the very thing that I relied on to establish a position of power in a relationship, and somehow, I had unwillingly relinquished that control. I had lost valuable leverage by not getting Markie to take me to her bed that night.

It made me uneasy, on edge. And the only way I could think of regaining some of my power was to spend time with another woman. To have a backup was my protection. Once I was flirting with Jean, being charming and seductive, Markie wouldn't matter anymore. Not in the least.

Jean met me at the Flowers Bar, which was my idea. A sick part of me was hoping that I'd run into Markie there, that I would nonchalantly smile, give a little wave, and then lean close to Jean and laugh as though we were having the best of times, as if to say, "See, I'm not *that* available, Markie."

But Markie never showed up. I couldn't imagine her going home on a Friday night at nine o'clock. Did she have another woman? Was she in bed with her right now? I looked across the table at Jean, one of the more desirable women in the community. She wore a royal blue silk blouse with a gold V-shaped pin at the neck, a dark vest and a tight blue skirt. Her dark short hair was cropped and spiked dramatically. Her tropical blue eyes stared directly into mine.

She was talking about the *very unfortunate*

situation between Lenny and me, how difficult it must be. She had a sincere look on her face, but I could read "I want to fuck you" in her eyes.

And frankly, that's the one way I can think of to make myself feel better when someone I want is in bed with someone else. I was anxious. It was after eleven and Markie still had not shown up.

I leaned closer to Jean. "I think you are a most extraordinary woman," I said in one of my sexier voices. "Don't misunderstand, this is *so* unlike me, but I just can't seem to stop thinking of holding you. I did not expect to have these feelings. I was just looking for a friend to help fill the lonely hours, as you so generously had suggested. And now, oh please don't take this wrong . . ."

Jean reached across the table, taking my hand in hers, "My place or yours?"

Chapter 10

I really thought Jean was out for a good time. How was I to know she was going to be one of those overly emotional women? I mean, she *did* call me. She knew I was the victim of a recent breakup. She should have realized the implications of a situation like that.

We went back to her house, and somehow I was given the role of the aggressor. Jean was playing it cool all of a sudden, as if she really was just trying to be a friend to me. I couldn't figure it. I had said I wanted to hold her. She offered to take me home.

Once we were in her apartment, she sat on the other side of the couch like she had no idea what was up. I thought she liked some kind of kinky sexual foreplay to get hot, the game where she pretends to be unaware of the sexual energy and somehow just gets taken. Actually, that's a favorite of mine, so I knew all the right moves.

I looked at her, sweet and shy, sitting at the other end of the couch and realized *I* was thinking about Markie, about how all I wanted to do was to fuck Jean so I didn't have to worry anymore about the strange feelings I'd been having since Markie had brought me home.

I stood up. I was tired of obsessing about Markie. Markie and I had had a wonderful time that evening. She undoubtedly had spent a small fortune on dinner alone, not to mention that small bottle of perfume. Only moments after finishing the hors d'oeuvres, she had excused herself from the table, saying that she had to use the restroom. It was wonderfully sweet of her to steal away to the small shop next door and return with the most elegant bottle of perfume I had ever seen — *Joueur* — a very expensive, unusual French perfume.

When she had pulled the curtains aside, she slid into the seat next to me, leaned over and whispered in my ear, "*Le Joueur pour un joueur.*" Shit. It's times like that when I wished I had paid more attention to the French I lessons at Washington High School and less time trying to look up Miss Triuette's dress. As I think back on it, there was one day I finally caught a glimpse of her lace white panties. That flash alone was worth missing the entire year of French.

Consequently, I had to surmise Markie was saying that the perfume and I had certain similarities, and since I'd never heard of a perfume with a derogatory name, I assumed I was being complimented.

"*Merci beaucoup.*" I was touched.

Markie opened the bottle, dabbed a small amount onto her finger, and ran her dampened fingertip from behind my ear down the V-neck of my sweater and barely between my breasts, leaving a moist trail of heady aroma.

"This is the fragrance that you wear only for me," she said, looking deep into my eyes. The small booth filled immediately with a scent alarmingly seductive.

"Of course, only for you," I replied, thinking that I already had this woman head over heels for me.

As I walked toward Jean, I could still smell the floral scent of that perfume. Thinking of Markie, only of Markie, I reached Jean, leaned over, and enclosed her with my body.

"I want you, Jean. You want me, too." I moved closer, taking her hair into my hands and pulling her towards me.

"I don't know," Jean said, reluctance clearly in her voice. "I really hadn't planned . . . I just wanted to . . ."

"Tell me that you haven't thought what it would feel like to have my fingers inside you? Tell me you don't want to let me give you pleasure."

"It's just that I don't usually . . . I mean, I have this problem of becoming emotionally involved so easily . . ."

So that's the game she wanted to play. She didn't want to be taken. She wanted to be sweet-talked.

"Jean, this isn't just a one-night stand for me. The time we've spent together tonight has made me feel extraordinarily close to you. I haven't had feelings like these in so long." That ought to get me somewhere, I thought.

"Really?" Jean purred.

"Really." I gave her one of my most sincere looks. I softly kissed her on the cheek. I guess our little conversation was the key to Jean's fantasy, because within seconds I had her blouse unbuttoned and my hands up her fashionable skirt.

Sometimes, when I'm put into the role of initiator, I have a tendency to go a little overboard with it. The fact that I look so feminine causes me to attract the butch, "I'll handle everything" types. So when the rare occasion arises when I'm making the moves, I tend to get carried away.

Jean lay back on the couch and I finished undressing her piece by piece. She did have a nice body, with small pointy breasts and exquisite pink nipples. I immediately flashed on Markie. I hadn't seen her naked, had no idea what her breasts looked like, let alone any part of her body. I longed to be with her at that very moment.

Jean was sighing. Without even realizing it, I had moved into automatic and was gently squeezing the pebble-like nipples.

"You are so beautiful," I said, flicking my tongue across a tiny hardened pellet.

I pulled my sweater over my head, allowing Jean to take a nice long look at my breasts — one of my finer assets, if I do say so myself. Hadn't Markie called them diamonds in the coal that night in the Flowers Bar? Her hands had been so strong, so confident as they caressed me. The sudden thought of Markie increased my arousal.

I leaned against Jean and began to brush my strawberry-colored nipples against her breasts. Such an intoxicating sensation, the silkiness of two women as they come into each other. She was watching each move I made, and I was in good form. It's exciting to me when I get to perform, when someone watches each movement I make and responds as if there is nothing quite as marvelous as being sexual with me.

Over and over I rubbed my breasts up against Jean. She squirmed under me saying things like, "You don't know how long it's been." As she was getting me hotter and hotter, I brought my mouth down to hers and licked her lips as if they were dipped in the Dom Perignon Markie had bought for me . . .

How exciting, how steamy Markie had been with her ability to play it cool. She had to have wanted to have sex with me that night. Seeing Jean respond made me certain of that fact. But Markie had sensed something different between us, something so much more than sexual! Markie did have quite a reputation — I'd heard it all after Lenny had done her research, and it was obvious that it would take quite a woman to nab Markie. The one who did would be well regarded in the community, that's for sure. And if I wasn't mistaking the direction our evening had taken, I was on my way to earning that respect.

"Oh yes, oh yes!" Jean was moaning. While I had been lost in thoughts of Markie, I had moved my hand down between Jean's legs and was pushing two of my fingers up against the small thin shaft between her down-covered lips.

She was wet. I slipped my fingers up and down between the crevice, enjoying watching her respond so dramatically. It didn't take much. A couple of quick flapping motions, a sudden penetration and I had Miss Jean right over the edge.

She hardly moved when she came, just bit her lower lip and made a small crying sound. I don't know what happened, but I had this unbearable urge to get the hell out of there. I looked down at her, and she stared back at me with one of those "you and I have a relationship now" looks. A classic look every lesbian I know has seen at least once in her sexual life.

"Ruby," Jean murmured as a small tear began to push its way down her cheek.

"Listen," I said, trying to be diplomatic. "I've got to be up early. I really should be heading out." I glanced at my watch. What if Markie had gone home after dinner? What if she had gotten into bed, unable to quit thinking about me, and tried to give me a call around eleven p.m.? And here I had been wasting my time with Jean who was already a little too much for my liking. Did the woman have to take things so seriously?

"Can I see you tomorrow?" she said, obviously distraught at my abrupt mood change.

"Uh . . . I don't really know what things are going to be like . . . me just being out of a relationship and all. Surely you can understand that?" God, I wanted out. I stood up.

"What about all those things you said about how you've felt feelings like you've never —"

"Listen, Jean," I said, cutting her off in mid-sentence. "There are no constants in life. In that moment, yes, I did feel those things. But that was then, this is now."

I pulled the sweater over my head. I guess I had been a little too harsh with her because her eyes suddenly filled with tears.

"Look, when things settle down in my life, I'll give you a call."

I walked to the door, forcing a thin smile onto my face. I wanted to get out of there without a scene. Jean said nothing, just sat there. I opened the door and hurried into the cool night air, thinking of Markie, only of Markie.

Chapter 11

There was no message from Markie on Ruby's answering machine that late evening when Ruby came rushing into her apartment. Nor did the call come all day Saturday . . . not that Ruby was waiting for the call, as she remarked casually to Carmen, who said she could not remember ever seeing Ruby so on edge.

"You've really been hooked by this woman, haven't you?" Carmen said, surprised.

"Look," Ruby replied almost too hastily, "Markie is an intriguing woman, there's no doubt about that, but I can assure you I'm not hooked!"

"Right, Rube . . . and when have I ever seen you just hang around the apartment on a Saturday?"

"I'm *certainly* not hanging —" A sharp ring issued from the doorbell. Ruby glanced at her watch — four-twenty p.m.

"Who could that be?" she said, opening the front door. On the front porch someone had placed a bouquet of the most delicate roses Ruby had ever seen. The petals were so fine they seemed to be dusted with lavender color. The glass vase burst with long-stemmed buds. Ruby brought the flowers towards her face, wanting only to relish their scent. A thin piece of stationery floated from between the roses to the floor. Ruby retrieved it.

"Perhaps there are many ways to court a woman such as you?" Ruby read. "Jefferson Park. Ten-thirty p.m. Wait in a Yellow Cab. Wear only a trench coat and the perfume. I prefer your hair up tonight, under a hat."

"Carmen!" Ruby shrieked, rushing back into the apartment. "Carmen! Carmen! Carmen! What did I tell you! The woman's crazy about me. Look at these roses! I know *these* roses. They're called Sterling Silver Roses. Expensive. They're something like thirty-five dollars for a half dozen, and there's . . . one, two, three, four, five, six, seven . . . Jesus! There are twenty-four roses here!"

"The woman's crazy all right," Carmen interrupted sarcastically.

"I just *knew* if I waited around today I would hear from her!" Ruby shot a quick glance at Carmen.

Carmen, who was her best friend, was also known to be a little loose with her tongue when it came to containing valuable information. Having Carmen as a friend had its advantages when Ruby needed to get the scoop on someone else, but Carmen was known to toot her horn in other orchestras, so to speak, and one thing Ruby *absolutely* did not want around the community was that she had been waiting around for Markie. She had told Carmen she was hot for Markie. Carmen had even dropped her off at Markie's office yesterday. No big deal. Ruby was always hot on somebody, *but waiting around? On a Saturday?* That bit of information in the wrong hands could be most damaging.

"Yeah, I knew if I waited around she'd make another attempt to win me over," Ruby amended.

"Sure," Carmen said nonchalantly. "Looks like you've got her good. What's the note say?"

Ruby set the roses down. "Now Carmen, a girl needs to keep some things private." Ruby grinned, slipping the note facedown under the vase.

Shit, she thought, if Carmen gets wind of this, half the community will be sitting at Jefferson Park tonight. Ruby went into the kitchen.

Carmen was not one to go out of her way to pry into other people's business, at least most of the time, but that note was too tempting. She used a nearby pencil to ease the note from under the vase of roses.

If I don't use my hands then I'm not really doing anything wrong, Carmen thought. Whatever the note said wouldn't matter to her anyway. Carmen quickly scanned the message, letting a low whistle escape from her lips. With the pencil she eased the note back into place.

"Do you like the vase?" Ruby asked as she returned to the living room carrying two steaming mugs. The long glass vase shimmered in the light.

"Great. Just great," Carmen said distractedly, wondering why Ruby wanted to keep secrets from her. Since when did Ruby refuse to share intimate details. Carmen prided herself on being one of the few women in this community who knew how to keep a secret! And now suddenly Ruby wanted to keep some things private?

Carmen couldn't wait to race to the pay phone at the corner of Washington and Van Ness to call Alise, just to get her opinion on the situation. After all, it wasn't really betraying a confidence if a note was left for her to read. Technically there was no confidence to be broken. Of course, if Ruby had thought to share the note with Carmen, had told Carmen that this was in the strictest of confidence, well that would have been a different matter altogether.

"Carmen? What's with you? Are you even listening? Can I borrow that trench coat of yours or not?"

"Sure," Carmen said, thinking she really didn't have any need for the coat tonight. After all, she and Alise could wear their short jackets.

Chapter 12

"You know," Carmen said, blowing her gum into a small symmetrical bubble, then popping it with her finger. A thin pink film adhered to her lips. "I haven't done something this bold in years. I guess it's the sort of thing one does when one's own life gets boring." She peered across the park toward the yellow cab sitting conspicuously under a street lamp at the front entrance of the park.

Carmen adjusted the collar on her black shirt and glanced in the rear view mirror. This wasn't the first time she and Alise had been involved in espionage. In their high school days, they had sat outside of the head cheerleader's home, dressed in dark inconspicuous clothing, hats pulled low over their long hair. They would wait, sometimes more than an hour, for the strawberry-blonde femme fatale to pass in front of an undraped bedroom window.

"We should get to see quite a show tonight. I suppose the whole Flowers Bar scene is going to be rated G compared to this, huh?" Alise rolled the car window down an inch or two.

"How'd *you* know about the bar thing?" Carmen said, shifting in the car seat to look at Alise directly. "That was supposed to be classified information. At least that's what Ruby said when she told me! Jesus! I used to be the only one she'd confide in. I can't figure out what's up with her lately!"

"Carmen," Alise said dryly. "*You're* the one who told me."

"Oh. Yeah. Well don't forget it goes no further than you!" Carmen said, glancing back to the taxi. A white Mercedes had just pulled up behind it.

"Here we go!" Carmen exclaimed, lifting the binoculars to her eyes.

Until that night, Carmen had only seen Markie from a distance. They didn't frequent the same night spots, didn't mingle with the same crowd. But there had been an occasion or two when Carmen had stopped by the Flowers Bar and noticed Markie. It seemed impossible to be in a room with Markie and not be seduced into watching her every move. Her actions were smooth, finely tuned, her allure not unlike that of a stallion as it galloped across a vacant field, penetrating a crisp spring breeze, nostrils flared, its mane lifting as it rode the wind. Unconquerable, Carmen thought.

Markie had a bodybuilder's frame. Rumor had it that she spent a considerable amount of time at the gym. Her jet black hair was cut short around her face, but it smoothly tapered into a small ponytail in the back. Carmen considered her very classy, always dressed as though she were ready for a photo shoot. She usually wore man-tailored sport jackets with expensive shirts. Eye-catching accessories, a gold hoop in one ear, black leather gloves, and a beguiling hat added to her well-known flair for style.

The word around the community was that Markie had had many lovers, and yet she was known to be very discriminating in her choice of bed partners. Almost every woman wanted to go out with her, as well as to have sex with her. Her reputation in that department was highly regarded and carefully scrutinized. The incident that occurred between Markie and Ruby in the Flowers Bar provided hours of juicy gossip-mongering. Everyone talked about it with the utmost discretion, since no one except Carmen was supposed to know the *exact* details. The thought of Markie following Ruby into the restroom and sucking her off on the sink made Carmen damp in her own panties.

Markie climbed out of the car and walked over to the taxi. She was talking to the driver, leaning down to the window. It took everything Carmen had to keep from starting the car and cruising closer to get a better look. If only she could hear the conversation.

Markie took a long drag on her cigarette and then tossed it to the ground, crushing the butt into the concrete.

"I like that," Carmen said in a low voice. "The way she handled that cigarette." There was something sensual in that erotic last deep puff, the disregard as the cigarette butt hit the street, the determination as Markie ground it into the cement.

"Yes. I see what you mean." Alise sighed as she watched through her own set of binoculars.

Markie climbed into the back seat next to Ruby. Carmen saw her lean over, bring Ruby's face close to her own as if she was whispering or kissing Ruby on the ear. The tail lights of the cab lit up, and the taxi started off into the night.

"Here goes," Carmen said as she started up her own car. "Our adventure begins."

The taxi sped through the streets, turning here, then suddenly turning again. There was a kind of determined desperation in the driver's technique. Carmen, not as adept in stunt-car driving, had a difficult time keeping up, let alone following. Inevitably she lost sight of the cab somewhere near Broadway and Van Ness.

"Shit!" She was crushed. "I can't believe I lost them!"

"Where do you think they could have gone?" Alise said, looking ahead, trying to spot the yellow cab further down Van Ness.

Carmen pulled over to the curb and leaned back. "Well, all I've got to say is that Ruby better let me in on what's gone down with her tonight, or I don't know how good a friend I'll be able to remain with her. Look at what she's put me through already, just from the very fact that she refused to share that note with me. I can't figure how she defines friendship anymore. Can you?"

"Carmen, not everyone can be as good a friend as you are."

Carmen blew another bubble and popped it quickly. "Isn't that the truth!"

The cab pulled in front of the Sappho Theater. Markie, who earlier had said, "Let's not talk just yet," turned to Ruby and broke the silence. "I want to excite you in ways you've never known." Her voice was warm, like maple syrup.

She helped Ruby out of the cab and walked her up to the ticket booth. Ruby had never been in the Sappho before, but was aware of what went on in there. Candace had told her about the explicit sex shows for women only, the private booths.

Ruby drew the trench coat closer around her body. A cool breeze caressed her legs and drifted up under her coat, causing her nipples to protest in sudden erection.

They entered the theater and walked down a blue-carpeted hallway until they reached room seventeen. Markie unlocked the door. The fragrance of musk escaped from the cozy room as the door drifted open. Ruby followed Markie in, sitting next to her on the black plush couch that faced a small raised stage.

Markie turned to Ruby and murmured, "You're all I've thought about since I dropped you off last night. How I've longed for you! Remembering the scent of you from when I had my tongue buried in you at the

Flowers Bar. I was up all night, thinking I had made a mistake in taking you home and not having you once again." Markie leaned forward and pressed a button on the low platform in front of them. Jazz music began to play.

"I know how —"

"Shh! Let me take care of everything, including the words."

Suddenly a slide door opened and a blonde walked into the room. She smiled seductively as she sat down on the platform directly in front of the two women.

"I'm Marisa," the woman purred as she slowly began to slide the strap of her black satin gown down one arm.

Markie turned to Ruby, lifting the hat from Ruby's head, letting the curls tumble down onto her shoulders. The sudden scent of *Jouer* encircled them both. "Hmm." Markie inhaled the intoxicating fragrance. "Very nice, very nice."

Marisa was teasing the border of the negligee up and across her claret red nipples — their color an exciting contrast to her fair skin, her silken blonde hair.

Candace had said that she and Annette had had sex in one of these private rooms with a woman they had never met before. Was this what Markie had planned for the evening? Markie was hard to figure. One moment she wanted to go slow with Ruby, the next she was setting up an orgy.

Ruby continued to watch Marisa run the lace border of her gown back and forth over her engorged nipples. The fabric seemed to scrape the hardened buds unmercifully as it scratched against the surface of the erect tissue.

"No," Markie whispered as though she had read Ruby's mind. "This isn't what you think. I still want to take my time with you, with us. It's just that last night, as I lay alone in bed, the thought of not making love to you was absolutely unbearable! Dear God, woman! There are so many ways I want to please you, like tonight . . . taking the time to arouse you. So often the most important senses are taken for granted during foreplay. Go ahead, take a look at Marisa — what a beauty she is. Have you ever seen nipples get so hard?" Markie unbuttoned the top button of the trench coat as she spoke, lightly running her warm tongue against Ruby's exposed neck.

Ruby felt a burning sensation deep between the moist lips of her pussy as she felt Markie's hot breath on her neck. Yes, she very much wanted another glimpse of those crimson nipples! How very taut they were as Marisa pulled that rough lace over the protruding tips! How very chafed!

"When you see a woman as pretty as Marisa," Markie continued, "it's hard not to wonder about her pussy." Markie's tongue circled up and around Ruby's ear. Licking, then darting her heated tongue into every crevice, Markie left behind a trail of warmth each place her tongue entered.

Marisa moved her hands from the top of the gown and slid them down the smooth satin to her slender waist, cupping her slightly rounded belly and gliding over her ample hips until she reached the gown's lace hem. With only the briefest hesitation, Marisa lifted the negligee ever so slightly, revealing the top border of a black silk stocking, a flash of her peachy thigh seemingly airbrushed with a light layer of flaxen hair, the black lacy strap from her garter belt. A saxophone wailed in the background.

"That's right. Pretend I had placed my tongue on that stunning pink pussy of yours," Markie said breathlessly, still trailing her tongue across Ruby's neck, down past her unbuttoned jacket collar. Markie pulled the trench coat open, exposing Ruby's own thighs. "Yes. There is nothing quite as arousing as what we can drink in with our eyes." Ruby felt Markie's hand barely touch the smooth texture of her thigh.

Ruby could not remember being so enflamed. Every part of her body was electrified. Markie teased her with her strong hands, barely touching her leg, yet not really making contact. And Marisa! Sitting only inches in front of her, Marisa raised that nightie unbearably slowly! Ruby wanted to see further up into that small space. She needed to look at the treasures buried beneath the satin veil.

As if Marisa could read Ruby's thoughts, she continued to raise the gown, fully unveiling the tops of both silk stockings, the long lace straps of the garter belt. Yet she kept her legs unforgivingly closed. For a brief instant, Ruby thought she could see a small patch of the golden fleece triangle as Marisa shifted, but that vision — or had it simply been a mirage? — evaporated rapidly.

Ruby's mouth was parched. And Marisa was so inviting, the damp well of her pussy only an effortless spreading-of-the-legs away! What was Marisa waiting for? Wasn't it obvious what this whole thing was about? Wasn't it time to continue this lesson of sensual foreplay?

"One thing I've learned," Markie said as she wet her finger with her tongue and ran the hot saliva across Ruby's lips, "is that each sense, independent of the others, can be incredibly powerful." She reached into her pocket and pulled out a long thick scarf. "Like the sense of smell. It's extraordinary how, on its own, without the demanding suggestions from sight and taste, smell perhaps can be the most erotic of all." She lifted the scarf up and around Ruby's eyes, securing it tightly behind Ruby's head.

"I really wouldn't mind blending sight *and* smell," Ruby said, alarmed that her chance to have a glimpse of Marisa's pussy had suddenly been robbed.

"Shh!" Markie exclaimed teasingly, guiding Ruby up from the couch even closer to Marisa. Ruby automatically was surrounded by the light musky fragrance so noticeable when they had first opened the door to room seventeen. It was the fragrance that Marisa wore, a simple scent, undemanding in its suggestiveness. The music suddenly stopped.

Markie pushed Ruby forward into a kneeling position, then turned her around. She groped the plush texture of the couch in front of her and heard a rustling as Marisa seemed to move from the platform to the couch directly in front of Ruby. Markie pulled her back gently so Marisa could situate herself, one leg on each side of Ruby's shoulders.

"Now, dear Ruby, I present to you the incredible sense of smell," Markie said, panting. "I'm going to move you, ever so slightly, forward . . . and at the very moment that you experience the first suggestion of Marisa's scent, I want you to say, 'Yes. Right here.' Are you ready?"

Ruby, overwhelmed with sexual tension, nodded.

"Good." Markie guided Ruby an inch at a time closer and closer to Marisa's open pussy.

Although Ruby was blindfolded, the closer she came to Marisa's pussy, the more easily she visualized every detail of it — the golden petal-like down-covered lips, the thickened clitoris too large to be contained. Ruby imagined it pushing its way from between those suffocating outer lips, the same surprising claret red as her nipples, as if that meaty tissue had been recently suckled.

As she moved closer, an intoxicating spicy aroma enveloped Ruby. She wanted only to tear off the blindfold, to feast her eyes on that golden triangle, those deep red cleaves of tissue! She wanted to bury her nose, her entire face, into that cherry-sweet pussy! "Yes. Right there," Ruby whispered desperately.

"Right there? Right there?" Markie said hotly. "This is where you can suck in her scent? Go ahead Ruby, take it in. Marisa, pull yourself apart. That's right, lift your ass up so Ruby can suck in every last bit of you!"

Ruby sensed Marisa pull the lips of her pussy apart, run her finger across her opened damp slit, and slide the thick sap over her protruding clitoris. Her finger seemed to flick back and forth, pausing occasionally to take yet another dip into the sugary well.

Ruby felt she was only inches from Marisa's red clit. She could envision Marisa's fingers as their quick motion fanned the pussy-sweet fragrance. Ruby took a deep breath. The aroma was staggering and she felt a shiver shoot through her body.

"Her pussy," Markie said hotly as if deeply aroused herself, "as you most probably would have expected, is the same scarlet red as her nipples. Can you imagine it? Such pale skin, such blonde hair, and yet she's the color of wine. Her clitoris is much thicker than I would have expected . . . for such a petite woman."

Ruby was so close that she actually could feel the breeze created by Marisa's non-stop whipping across her clitoris.

"And then there's sound . . ." Markie panted. "Listen to Marisa as she drives that flap back and forth. Just listen to that!" The room was quiet except for the amplified slapping sound as Marisa increased the rhythm of the beat across her engorged clit.

"And finally, there is touch." Markie lifted the back of Ruby's trench coat, forcing two fingers into Ruby's tight wet opening. She pushed them in, without regard for the fact that with each penetration, Ruby's face was being submerged into Marisa's own honey pot. Markie lunged, sinking her fingers into Ruby's very depths as Ruby's face sunk into the luscious Marisa. Ruby lapped wildly, trying to angle her nose in such a way as to enter Marisa with it, all the while imagining — using smell, sound, touch, taste — what that delicious pussy must look like.

Ruby bent over, Markie taking her again and again from behind. Marisa arched up, jamming herself against Ruby's desperate tongue. The hot scent of musky spice filled the room. Suddenly Ruby erupted into a crimson orgasm. She grabbed Marisa's legs, fucking her harshly with her tongue as Markie herself began to moan in pleasure.

Within seconds the room became surprisingly silent. Markie watched Marisa pull herself up and reach for the hundred-dollar tip Markie passed to her. Marisa mouthed the words: "I'll see you later, sweetie," and exited through the door she had entered earlier.

Markie turned Ruby toward her, untied the scarf, and lightly ran her tongue across Ruby's lips, tasting the familiar sweetness of Marisa. She glanced at her watch. She had just barely enough time to get Ruby home and be back in time to pick up Marisa when her shift ended. It had been far too long since she had had Marisa.

Chapter 13

Carmen and I went back the long way. We had been friends about ten years, and basically, I pretty much accepted Carmen's faults, that is up until the time I started seeing Markie. I'm not sure exactly how the whole thing came about except that Carmen started demanding too much from me.

I'm not one to keep secrets from my close friends — that's not my style, especially if I've grown to trust them. But when I started seeing Markie, frankly I didn't want to talk about it because I was afraid I'd jinx it. Now where the hell that kind of thinking even came from, I'll never know, because I'm not superstitious and it was usually the woman *I* was seeing who worried that she somehow was going to jinx things. I'd usually just sail along.

Maybe I was secretive because Markie was considered the hottest woman in town and she was interested in me. I thought she was falling head over heels for me. If *that* wasn't good for my standing in the community, I don't know what else was.

So I wanted to try to play it cool, as if seeing Markie was no big deal. She was spending all kinds of money on me, talking about how very special, how very different I was.

Playing it cool, I thought. So when Carmen started badgering me for information about what was going on between Markie and me, I just couldn't oblige her. She wanted to know every move, every feeling. I had to create a boundary. And do you think my closest buddy Carmen was going to give me a little breathing space? *No way!* She was like a leech, trying to suck out every last detail.

I tried to explain that sometimes a woman needs a little time to process things herself, that it has nothing to do with best friends. But Carmen didn't seem to hear any of that.

Or maybe the whole final falling-out was really about jealousy . . .

It all started the day after my second date with Markie. She had taken me to this women's club. I don't remember ever having had that kind of sex before. It was all pretty private, personal. And, I swear to God, I got home at two in the morning and my phone was ringing as I walked in the door.

I was pretty high. First, I had had the most

incredible orgasm, and second, I was sure that Markie was starting to fall for me. She told me on the way home that she wanted me for herself, that I inspired her to act upon fantasies she had never dared dream, and that she had always envisioned finding a woman like me. She didn't have to say those things because we had already had sex, so it wasn't like she was trying to get me into bed. I've always felt that it was the "after sex" conversation that pointed in what direction the relationship was really going to head.

So the phone was ringing. Two in the morning and I'm thinking it must be some sort of an emergency. I picked up the phone, my heart pounding, and who the hell do you think it was? That's right, good ol' Carmen letting me know she needed her trench coat in the morning. That was her excuse for the call.

She then casually steered the conversation to my date. Why did I need a trench coat? Where'd I go?

"Carmen," I said, slightly aggravated. "I'm really tired. And like I told you yesterday, I'm trying to maintain a sense of privacy."

I could hear the anger in her voice. "What's all this privacy shit with you all of a sudden? Huh? It used to be me and you no matter what! What's the matter? You starting to think you're a little too good for your old friends now that you and Markie —"

"Carmen," I interrupted. "I'm just trying to —"

"Yeah, yeah. No sense wasting who you are on good ol' Carmen, right? That is, until you need a ride, or a trench coat, or your faucet fixed!"

Now that was Carmen for you. Whenever we had a spat, she always brought up that damned faucet she fixed for me three years ago. I swear, these butch girls do you a favor and they brand it into their memory.

"Look Carmen, come on over tomorrow, I'll fix us some breakfast. We can talk then." I thought that would appease her temporarily.

At eight o'clock the next morning, guess who shows up at my door with a big picnic basket? Markie. I can't tell you how surprised I was to find her standing there. She looked intoxicating, holding a bottle of champagne, a bouquet of blue carnations, the Sunday paper.

What was I supposed to do? Turn her away? In my opinion, the true test of a friendship is to be able to cancel plans with your buddy at the last minute because you got something hot going on with a new lover. That's basic, isn't it? So I showed Markie in, and excused myself momentarily to call Carmen. As luck would have it, there was no answer. Oh well. My opinion? The second true test of a friendship is to be able to turn your buddy away at the door without too much of a hassle.

The fantasy was this: the doorbell rings, I answer it. It's Carmen. I whisper with a smile that I'm sort of busy at the moment . . . wink, wink. Carmen, my best friend, is always happy when my life is going good. She winks back and says with a grin, "I'll call you later."

Markie gave me a hug. "Breakfast in bed!" she said, glancing around my apartment for a sign as to where the bedroom was. God, this woman was so hot I could barely stand it. I couldn't believe she showed up the next morning. She was crazy about me, I could just feel it! We hugged each other and we walked arm-in-arm down the hall to my bedroom. Just as we landed on the bed the doorbell rang. Guess who.

I walked to the door, practicing my wink, and opened it with a smile.

"Hey!" Carmen says handing me a bag of bagels. "I'm ready for some serious eating. P.M.S."

"Ah, Car," I whispered motioning toward the bedroom with a wink. "I'm sort of busy right now." I threw a second wink in for emphasis, since by the look on Carmen's face, the first one wasn't having any effect.

"What the hell is that supposed to mean? Am I mistaken or did we have plans this morning?"

"Well, there's been a sudden setback. I tried to call but you had already left."

Carmen looked at me angrily and said in a low voice, "Noooo fucking problem! Need anything fixed before I leave?"

"Oh come on, Carmen," I responded. "Is that all you think there is to our friendship?" Although my toilet *had* been making a funny leaking noise lately, and I had planned to drop it into the conversation over breakfast, but I realized it would have been pretty tacky of me to mention it at that particular moment. At least, that was my general feeling.

"Friendship? You call this friendship?" Carmen shot me a harsh glance and turned away.

"Carmen, please . . ." I tried to keep the irritation out of my voice. She could be so dramatic at times. She didn't acknowledge me. She kept right on walking around the side of the building and out of sight.

Jeez, I thought, shaking my head, closing the front door. I wondered if, when the timing was right, Markie would mind taking a look at that toilet.

Chapter 14

"So, do you like this Ruby or what?" Sal said, leaning forward and stirring her tea that was still to hot to sip.

"Yeah, I like her, from the standpoint that she's a player too. And knowing this community, word's probably spread around that we're seeing each other."

"I've got to admit, the two of you are a pretty hot-looking item." Sal shrugged.

"But as you well know, my dear Sal," Markie said coolly, "I'm *not* looking for a teammate. Ruby is a challenge. And *therein* lies the attraction. Once I've had her, once it's known that she's fallen for me . . ."

"Hmm," Sal said, lifting the mug to her lips. "I wouldn't mind seeing the two of you in action. She pretty hot in bed?"

Markie waved to the waitress, motioning for the check. "That woman has a . . . How can I put this without being crude? I've been with a lot of women, a lot of beautiful women, and I've never seen a pussy quite like hers."

"Oh yeah?" Sal said leaning closer. "And how is that?"

"Well, I was thinking . . ."

Ruby could hear the phone in the bedroom ringing, but her hands were submerged in the toilet tank. "Shit!" she said aloud as she tried to screw the large bulb back into place. The damn thing had come off so fucking easily, so easily that Ruby actually had decided that the toilet would be simple enough to fix herself. That had been one hour and four overflows ago. Now all she wanted to do was get the pieces back where they had originally been in the first place. That rubber cap with the chain? She had thought she had seen the chain part hanging off that little hook, but then when she flushed the toilet again, it overflowed. She remembered that Lenny had once stuck a plunger in the toilet for that, and Ruby had even attempted to use the plunger herself, to no avail. With each flush the water poured over the top of the toilet bowl. What had been a minor tinkling sound had become a nightmare thanks to Ruby's fix-up job. She could never quite understand the whole plunger theory anyway. How sticking a pole with a large cup on the end and pushing ever really did anything. Didn't make sense in the past and certainly didn't make sense now. She yelled aloud, "God damn you, Carmen!"

The telephone rang a third time before the answering machine clicked on. Ruby could hear Markie's voice over the constant sound of running water. Her toilet refused to stop.

"Hey, dear Ruby, I was out having a cup of tea, thinking of you . . ."

Ruby pulled her hands out of the tank, drying them haphazardly on her jeans, and walked to the phone.

". . . hoping that you'd have some time for me this afternoon. Give me a call when you get in. All I can think of is you . . ." The machine clicked off.

Ruby stared at the phone. That's right, she thought, I'm *not* that available. She replayed the message. Just the sound of Markie's voice made her tremble.

Candace had called earlier and mentioned that she thought she had seen Markie leaving the Sappho with some blonde late last Saturday night. And even though Ruby knew one hundred percent that Candace must have been mistaken, there was a small place inside her that felt a wee bit uncomfortable. Could Markie have dropped her off and returned to spend the rest of the night fucking that . . . that woman? After that taxi ride home, the things Markie had said to her? Impossible. If Markie had been in the mood for sex, she would have slept with Ruby. Not some prostitute like Marisa . . . Marisa with the incredibly red nipples, with the intoxicatingly scented pussy . . .

"I'm certain you're mistaken," Ruby said smoothly into the phone, concentrating on keeping her voice steady. "Markie spent the night with me. We had brunch the next morning." And of course, Carmen could confirm that part.

"Annette and I were leaving the movie theater across the street and, well, it sure *looked* like Markie opening the door to that white Mercedes, letting that woman in. But you know how difficult it can be to see clearly late at night and all," Candace said casually. "You got a thing for her now?"

"She's hot, no question about that," Ruby replied. "And I'm sure she's fallen for me. But do I have a thing for her? I don't know, Candace. I'm not sure where I want the relationship to go at this point." Ruby was still distracted. There was no way Candace could have seen Markie. No way at all. After all, hadn't Markie shown up the very next morning, only hours after she had dropped Ruby off? Surely she had gone home and slept. The breakfast, the champagne, the flowers, the tender lovemaking after the meal . . . there was no way that could have been *her* Markie.

Even so, as Markie was leaving the message on the answering machine, Ruby had a sudden urge to play hard-to-get. Since when did she feel so needy for someone? She figured she'd wait a while, and then maybe, if she was so inclined, she'd give Markie a call.

Ruby went back to the toilet that had now mysteriously stopped running. Good. It was fixed. She replaced the porcelain lid on the back tank. See, she thought, I can take care of things perfectly fine on my own.

She picked up a small square of toilet paper that had fallen to the floor, dropped it into the bowl, and flushed the toilet. Within seconds the entire bathroom was once again flooded with water.

"Hello, Markie?" Ruby purred into the answering machine, her feet still wet, plunger still in hand. "Do you think you can come help me with an itsy bitsy problem?"

Chapter 15

"There," Markie said with a satisfied smile. "This toilet just needed some fine tuning."

Ruby crossed the room, giving Markie a warm embrace. "What would I ever do without you?"

"Precisely." Markie kissed Ruby on the cheek. "I'm trying to make myself indispensible. One of the oldest ploys, but effective. Or so I've been told."

"Yes." Ruby whispered, her lips brushing Markie's mouth.

Markie pressed her mouth against Ruby's, tracing her tongue carefully around the moist entrance.

"Ruby, I know we've only been seeing each other for a short time, but each moment I spend with you brings me in closer and closer. Do you understand what I'm trying to say to you?"

Ruby could feel Markie's firm body surrounding her. She felt overcome with the desire to simply melt into Markie. Never having experienced a bonding such as this with any other lover, she had a sudden need to attach herself to Markie and never let go.

Markie, running her tongue down Ruby's neck, whispered her need for Ruby. She had never wanted a woman so desperately, she said, lifting Ruby's T-shirt, sliding her hands up and pushing them roughly over Ruby's pert breasts.

"Do you feel the same as I do?" Markie said, her voice trembling, her breath hot.

"Markie," Ruby whispered, pulling Markie tight into her arms. "I'm very frightened. I need to tell you this. I just haven't ever —"

"Shh." Markie lifted Ruby and carried her to the bed. "Let me show you how very much I love you."

"Love me? You love me, Markie? How could you possibly know . . . we've hardly . . ."

"Ruby, sweet Ruby," Markie said, lying down next to Ruby on the bed, cradling Ruby in her arms. "Did anyone ever tell you that you think too much? Sometimes we can analyze all the true feelings out of something if we try hard enough."

Markie propped herself up on her elbows, leaning over Ruby. "I know myself quite well." She twisted one of Ruby's soft curls between her fingers. "I've been with many women, Ruby. I know what's what when it comes to feelings. And yes, I've had my share of infatuations. I'm sure you have too. But Ruby, when emotions such as what I have for you emerge, it's a totally different thing. There's no need for me to wait to 'get to know you better.' I know you. Deep in the very heart of me, I know you, woman. You'll think this is crazy, but I believe we were lovers from another life who have found each other once again. Haven't you ever had the same sense? That we've known each other for centuries? It just seems so familiar, so right."

Ruby had closed her eyes, soaring on each word as it floated from Markie's lips. Yes, she thought. An ancient love, lovers for centuries. No wonder she had felt so lost, so out of control with her own feelings.

"Let me love you. Please let go and let me have you completely." Markie was no longer raised above Ruby. She had slowly worked her way down to Ruby's abdomen and was tonguing a trail of wet circles around Ruby's navel.

"Oh Markie," Ruby moaned. "Yes. I so much want to let go"

Markie pulled Ruby's skirt down, continuing the butterfly flutters with her tongue. Her hand slid down from Ruby's curved hip. Markie placed her fingers into the woven curly hair that decorated Ruby's pussy.

"I want to know every part of you," Markie said as she moved Ruby down to the edge of the bed, angling her in such a way that the light from the window hit directly onto Ruby's throbbing pussy.

Markie knelt on the floor and spread Ruby's legs apart.

"You are so beautiful," Markie exclaimed. She grabbed a hand mirror from the night stand and handed it to Ruby. "This right here," Markie said as she separated the lips, "is perhaps the most extraordinary treasure I've ever seen."

Ruby held the mirror so she could watch Markie begin her slow exploration. Markie lifted the lips apart and traced her finger lightly over the pink, wrinkled flesh.

"Here is the place where the dark hair ends, right on the innermost curve of the large lips," Markie said breathlessly. "I like this, where the hair stops and the smooth skin begins." She ran her fingertip along the fringed border of the right lip.

"Oh, and then all these creases!" Markie moved her finger into the furrowed skin that was becoming a deeper watermelon color.

Her finger followed the thick flesh down to the small inner lips. Markie took the lips, one in each hand and tugged down on them, stretching the entire clitoral pouch. Ruby gasped in response as the sensation intensified.

"Do you like the way this feels, Ruby? The way I can just draw down on these little flaps and get your entire clitoris to respond?"

Ruby sighed. She watched Markie make each quick, gentle yank on the fleshy folds.

Releasing the petite, handlebar-like lips, Markie's fingertip skated to the gorgeous opening of Ruby's hot cunt. The slit was glazed with a coating of oily jelly. Markie dipped her fingers into the well and then brought them up toward her face, rotating the two lubricated fingers over each other, then painting her own lips with the sugary sap.

"Mmmm," she moaned. She ran her tongue across

Ruby's sweetness. She dipped her fingers once again into the wet entrance and then smeared the buttery gel across Ruby's thimble-shaped nipples.

Greedily, Markie latched onto a nipple with her mouth and began sucking, placing three fingers back into the slippery cavern.

Ruby lifted her hips, rested her feet on the bed's edge, spread her legs as wide as possible. The intense heat from the sun beat down on her pussy.

Markie increased the suction on the hardened nipple as her fingers moved deep into Ruby.

Ruby arched her hips up higher. "Please," she panted. "Pull your fingers out of me real slow."

Markie could sense that Ruby was no longer in control. The past few times, when close to orgasm, Ruby would begin mumbling, her words seeming to slide into each other, not quite comprehensible. But this morning, Markie noticed a change. The mumbling was becoming discernible. Markie felt an undeniable surge of power.

Ruby mumbled incoherently for a brief instant, then said quite clearly, "Yes. Pull them out real slow! Slower! That's right. Now hook your fingertips. Hook them so they skim across the top of my cunt. Yes. Please! Scrape them! Scrape them! No! Slower. Slower!"

She was demanding now. Markie tugged her fingers, millimeter by millimeter, out from Ruby's cunt. Clamping as tightly as possible, Ruby tried desperately to grasp Markie's fingers, to hold them in place.

The pressure from Markie's hooked fingers as she carefully dragged them across the small raised rough area on the ceiling of Ruby's pussy must have been too much. Ruby clutched fistfuls of Markie's hair as she pounded into orgasm.

"I love you! I love you! I love you!"

Sal pulled away from the bedroom window and leaned against the brick exterior of the apartment complex. She ran her fingers through her hair. The sun was hot, very hot indeed.

Chapter 16

Since Carmen and I were no longer on the best of terms, I started spending more time with Candace. Candace's favorite greeting seemed to be, "I hate to be the one to tell you this but . . ." The incident with Jean was a case in point. Candace wasted no time calling to inform me that Jean was assassinating my character, saying to anyone who would listen that I had seduced and then abandoned her, that I had insinuated that Jean and I had a chance for a relationship but I walked out as soon as I was sexually satisfied.

I don't mind if someone talks about me if that's what she needs to do, but the fact was I walked out as soon as *Jean* was satisfied. After all, I do have a reputation to keep intact! God, the bitterness some women carry around!

I basically liked Candace, and, as I've often said, I try to accept other people's shortcomings. For example, Candace has a habit of bearing unpleasant news. I wondered if she derived some type of enjoyment from the response she would get after spreading potentially damaging gossip. So, not wanting to give her that satisfaction, I did my best to act nonchalant whenever she had information I needed "for my own good."

I'm bringing this up because during the first two months I was dating Markie, Candace made innuendoes that Markie wasn't to be trusted. At first it was casual, like when she said she had seen Markie leaving the Sappho with that blonde. But her information seemed to be coming in at a steady pace. Markie was seen here, she'd say. Did I know anything about a woman named Sandra? Was it true that Markie never settled for one woman?

Every time Candace would issue another communique, I'd listen to what she had to say, let it sift through my mind, compare it to the Markie *I* knew and the intimacy that we shared, and basically discard ninety-nine percent of the exaggerations. There were a few times, however, when a nagging doubt would linger even after I had appraised the whole situation. Consequently, I would end up turning an ugly little detail over and over in my mind until it got to the point I could barely sleep at night.

That's when I decided I was going to have to take *the* big risk with Markie. There's a certain point in every relationship where playing it cool becomes passé. I believed Markie and I were getting close to that place. We were seeing each other three to five times a week, I reasoned. Markie had showered me with an incredible amount of cards, flowers, gifts. The sex which had started out as a hot good time was now evolving into intimate lovemaking. If I wasn't able to talk to Markie now, if I couldn't open up to her about my need for her, my insecurities, my desire for a commitment, when would I *ever* be able to?

Chapter 17

"I don't know if we should have picked that movie tonight," Ruby said as Markie opened the door to her apartment.

"I thought you enjoyed it, sweetie," Markie replied. She took Ruby into her arms.

"I just feel so emotional now." Ruby snuggled closer to Markie.

"You've been quiet the whole evening," Markie said, gently guiding Ruby to the plush softness of the living room couch. "There's something else, besides the movie, isn't there?"

Ruby turned away. She was overwhelmed by her incredible need for Markie. Never, ever, had she felt so out of control, so vulnerable! What if Markie wasn't serious about her? What if Markie laughed at Ruby? Made a fool of her?

"Ruby." Markie took Ruby's chin in her hand and turned Ruby toward her. "Look at me," she said as she encircled Ruby with her arms. "My God, you're like a frightened little bird! What is it? Please. If you can't share what you're feeling with me, then somehow I've failed you."

This is it, Ruby thought. She was exhausted from carrying the burden of her insecurities. She wanted to make a true commitment, one from deep in her heart. Being loved by Markie these last few months had opened up a part of her she had never experienced before, almost as if the missing piece to her soul had been found through Markie with love, support, and warmth. Ruby had never had a lover burrow her way into the very core of her. It was almost as if Markie had become an extension of Ruby's life force itself.

"It's okay, Ruby, you can trust me." Markie ran her fingers through Ruby's tangled curls.

"Markie," Ruby said, feeling a small tear tickle the corner of her eye and spill over the lash onto her cheek. "I'm very scared. I'm in love with you in such a desperate way. It's just that I'm starting to feel defenseless. I know you, but do I really? I hear stories, Markie. People call me just to tell me rumors. I don't know . . ." A teardrop, larger than the first, repeated the journey of its predecessor, followed by another and then another. "I know how it is when we're together, the things you say, the way you make love to me . . . and I hardly pay any attention to most of those dreadful stories I hear. But sometimes a phrase or something will stick in my mind and I'll keep thinking about it over and over . . ."

"Anything, anything you want to ask me, you do it. There will always be stories. People like you and me, women who are watched, always generate a certain amount of mystique, a certain amount of exaggerated history. It's all invented, hearsay. I have *nothing* to hide from you, my precious."

"Are we . . . are we committed to each other? We've never really said those words. I assumed it was just you and me, but then I realized I had no business doing such a thing! You could have other women you're doing the same thing with."

"Is that what you think? Is that what you really think, Ruby?" Markie's voice was stronger, louder. "Get something straight, woman. I don't make love to you the way I do and then go have other women on the side! A commitment? You're worried about that because we haven't said those words? Well here, here, here . . ." Markie tugged the diamond pinky ring off her finger and placed it onto Ruby's. "Here's your commitment. You and me. No others. Let them talk, let them call you every day with a story about me. Let them call you twice a day, three times a day. It won't matter, will it? No one sees the way it is between you and me, do they? No one could possibly grasp the depth of my love for you . . . except for you. You know it, don't you, Ruby? Are *you* ready to make a commitment with me?"

"Yes, yes!" Ruby said, the tears flowing down her cheeks.

"Then we won't worry anymore about anyone else but you and me. And you might want to consider who these so-called 'friends' are, trying to sabotage the best thing you've ever had."

Yes, Ruby thought. Some friends they've been!

Chapter 18

You know, the more I thought about it, the clearer my life became. My friends were fun to hang out with, but were they *really* pleased that I was happy? After Markie and I made the commitment to each other, I spent less time worrying about what Markie was doing and more time assessing my relationship with my friends. Carmen and I were no longer in contact. What a fair-weather friend she turned out to be. And Candace had called several times wanting to see a movie or have a bite to eat, but I had a better understanding what her real motives were.

Markie's point was well-taken when she said that the way to tell a *true* friend is how she treats you when you're happy. Everybody likes to commiserate with a buddy who's down and out — for a while anyway. But when it comes to happiness, Markie warned, watch how many of your friends will try their best to ruin it for you. And that's the category I found myself placing Candace in more often than not.

The evening I arrived home with Markie's diamond-smothered pinky ring on my finger, Candace called. The call was typical of her, I realized, when I had a chance to think it over. I was floating, had never felt better. I told her about the ring. I don't even think she heard me because she went right into a detailed account of how someone had told someone who told her that Markie had been seen the night before last at some . . .

I cut her off mid-sentence. "Stop! Just stop!" I snapped into the phone. "I'm tired of this! It's 'friends' like you that I need to weed out of my life!"

"What's that supposed to mean?" Candace said sharply.

"Just what I fucking said." I was out of control, suddenly blaming all of my past doubts and insecurities on her. "Here I am in the best relationship I've ever had, my first real commitment, and all you can do is tear it apart!"

"Oh please!" Candace said sarcastically. "All of a sudden Ms. 'Love them till the next one comes along' has got herself a real commitment! Who the fuck do you think you're talking to? Huh? I'm about the last friend you have left! Here I am, risking the friendship to keep you from going under on what is definitely a sinking ship and all you can do is tell me to fuck off! Well, good luck to you, sister! See who's around to rescue you when you're drowning!"

She slammed the phone down in my ear. Just as well, that bitch. Some friends I had chosen!

Chapter 19

Ruby's solitary descent into the labyrinth of love eventually led to her downfall. Subtly at first, Ruby fell deeper and deeper into the web, slowly giving self and soul away to Markie.

It was true that what she experienced in this relationship was like nothing she had ever encountered before. Markie, and only Markie, filled her thoughts. She would find herself, during the workday, sitting at her desk, staring into the ring's diamonds as they sparkled vividly under the fluorescent lights. She lost herself in sweet daydreams — Markie's strength as she carried Ruby into the bedroom; the heat that radiated from Markie's body as they lay, naked in each other's arms; Markie's whispered "forever" and "always."

Their relationship was exactly as Ruby had always fantasized. Ruby had found *the* woman who had entered her life and swept her away, the woman who filled her so completely she never needed to have an affair again, never needed to hang onto her stuffed bear and let the tears of her empty grief soak its furry face.

And since her Princess Charming had finally arrived, Ruby no longer needed anything or anybody else. Ruby's life was taking a turn. She didn't socialize with her friends anymore or keep an eye out for another woman to take Markie's place. She spent her free time either with Markie or thinking about her. It seemed to be enough. That she was no longer on speaking terms with her closest friends didn't matter. She had Markie as a best friend. Ruby declined dinners and movies with her work buddies. She had Markie to see movies with. For flirting, and lovemaking, and sharing secrets, and for just about anything else that Ruby could imagine, she had Markie.

Ruby gave herself away to her lover, sacrificed her being in the name of love. She cast independence aside in the hopes of merging, bonding into another person's identity, believing Markie's essence would fill her eternal emptiness.

But Ruby was unwilling to take the harrowing journey deep inside herself. In truth, only *one* woman would ever be able to quench the fire of loneliness that burned within her. That woman stood, staring back at Ruby with haunted eyes, waiting to be recognized, as Ruby looked past her in the mirror and wondered if she was indeed pretty enough.

Chapter 20

"I don't think I want to do that with Ruby." Markie leaned back in the lounge chair and adjusted her visor in an attempt to shield the demanding sun from her eyes.

"Hey," Sal replied. "Is this the same Markie who only a few weeks ago was talking all this shit about playing Ruby? So where'd you come up with a conscience all of a sudden? Has Miss Ruby somehow worked her way into the master's heart? Has Markie been caught in her own web?"

Markie was silent. The intensity of the heat made

even a simple response seem to require an extraordinary amount of energy. A light film of perspiration moistened her fingertips as she slid them down her arm to her naked pinky finger where the missing diamond ring once sat.

She was tired of Sal, tired of having to answer her questions. And what was it now? Was Sal's life so dull that Markie had to act as the entertainment committee? When was the last time Sal had come to her with something interesting in her own life to share? Sal suddenly bored her. It was barely worth the effort to explain why she didn't want to play out Sal's latest fantasy.

"Oh really, Sal!" Markie said, not bothering to hide the irritation in her voice. "Must your excitement revolve around the women I'm fucking? Can't you find someone on your own to play with?"

"Excuse me!" Sal said sarcastically. "My, we're a little touchy today."

Markie muttered an apology as she loosened the tie from her halter top and pulled it aside to expose her firm breasts.

Despite the fact that Sal had seen her naked many times, Markie noticed Sal's once-over as she stole another look at Markie's perfect body. Markie was a body-builder, and she knew Sal was envious of her ability to take off her clothes and know that everyone would admire her strong curves and full muscles that emerged gracefully from beneath her tight, tanned skin.

Markie knew she had an incredible body. There was no question about that. But she also knew that what turned Sal on was her attitude, her mind. Sal just loved to listen as Markie explained what she was planning, how she was going to get what she wanted. And without a doubt, Markie always ended up with the prize.

"Okay, so you don't want to set Ruby up for that scene," Sal said. "It doesn't mean anything, not really. It's just that this is the first time you've refused to include a woman you're playing in some of our action. That's all, no big deal . . ."

"How can you say that! What was it — two, three weeks ago you stood outside the window while I laid Ruby out for you?" Markie sat up and turned to face Sal. She felt an unexpected defensiveness. "Just because I'm not in the mood to share her in *your* sex fantasy, you've got it in your head that I'm —"

"Okay! Okay!" Sal said quickly. "I was thrown off guard. You've never said no to me before, that's all. The stuff I said about Ruby in your heart? I was just playing around, you know, bullshit talking. No problem. I know, in fact everyone knows, that you'll never be entrapped by a woman. After all, you *are* the master of the game."

"Yes. The master. And no one will ever take me in, play me for a fool. No one!"

Markie relaxed in the lounge chair. She needed a moment to think, to sort things through. She had felt disoriented, out of control. What could she have possibly been thinking? To come off so protective of Ruby! There had been a sudden desire to possess, to cherish Ruby when Sal had suggested doing that sex scene, but it had only been momentary. God! Even Sal had suspected it. Markie had become too careless with Ruby. She glanced at her pinky finger. She'd never, ever given a ring to a woman. What the hell had come over her? She needed to take care of Ruby before the situation got out of hand. Imagine if word got out that Markie had fallen, been taken in by . . . She sat up and shook her head.

"Sal!" Markie said, rising from the lounge chair. "You still got that Lara's phone number?"

Sal leaned back in the lounge chair, basking in the sun's steady heat. Markie had hurried into the house to call Lara, which was just fine as far as Sal was concerned.

Sal had always fantasized about being in a relationship with Markie, but it had never happened. They were best friends. They shared a lot of stories, but not once had Markie even attempted to make a play for Sal. Over the years, Sal had watched Markie fuck many women and had even been involved in many of the sex scenes Markie had orchestrated, but in Sal's mind, it was a partnership with Markie she really wanted.

Sal had waited patiently as Markie went from one conquest to the next. She anticipated the day when Markie finally grew tired of the game and turned to her for real love. But suddenly, Sal's strategy was being jeopardized by Ruby, who was having an unusual effect on Markie.

If I can't have Markie's heart, Sal thought as she adjusted the sun visor over her eyes, there's no way I'm letting someone else take it.

"Yes!" Markie called from the kitchen window, interrupting Sal's thoughts. "It's Lara in an hour!"

Sal turned to Markie and gave her a thumbs-up signal.

"That's my Markie," Sal muttered. She let out a sigh of relief. It seemed as though Ruby wouldn't be that big a problem after all.

Chapter 21

I swear, once I got that ring on my finger, nothing else in the world seemed to matter except Markie. It was the most extraordinary feeling to be filled so completely by someone. It was all I had ever fantasized about! Until Markie, I had been disenchanted with the idea of love everlasting. How many times had I attempted to capture it, to no avail? And now, unexpectedly, I had developed a rejuvenated perspective on love!

About a year before I met Markie, I read a book about soul mates. It made reference to a special person out in the world, somewhere, who would fit into the empty place in my heart just like the last puzzle piece slides into a jigsaw puzzle. That, I thought, was exactly how Markie meshed into me.

Love! It was glorious! I had always dreamed it would be like this! *I* was one of the very few lucky ones who had been chosen in this lifetime to find my spiritual partner. I was not foolish enough to ignore this fate. I felt a deep sorrow for all of my friends who had been searching so long for the true love I had been fortunate enough to find. No wonder they were envious! No wonder they lacked understanding, ready to destroy what Markie and I had found!

I turned the ring on my finger, watching as the sunlight reflected the diamonds and then broke into a sprinkling of rainbows around the interior of my car. I pulled into Markie's driveway and parked.

There was no answer when I rang the bell, which was strange because Markie and I had planned to meet at four and I was already twenty minutes late. I glanced around the side of the house. Perhaps Markie was in the backyard, still sunbathing with Sal.

There were two lounge chairs, Markie's sun visor, and a magazine. At the back door, I gave a firm rap. Nothing. I knocked again. "Markie?"

She had probably run out to get wine, flowers, maybe even pâté. It would be just like her to think of some romantic touch. I reached under the potted plant where Markie kept the spare key, only to discover it was missing. Assuming that Markie would arrive any moment, I returned to the front porch and sat on the top step.

I checked my watch. Another fifteen minutes had passed. She was over a half hour late. What could have happened? I twisted the diamond ring on my finger, beginning to worry. What if she had gotten into a car accident? I felt a deep anxiety pass through me. I could *never* survive without Markie. It would be too much! And who would be there to offer loving support as I grieved for her? I had no friends anymore. A sudden loneliness swept through me. I couldn't stand it. I had to get home. Maybe Markie had called, left a message on the machine — a mixup of some sort! I hurried back to the car and raced home.

Chapter 22

A half hour had passed since Markie arrived at Pierre's restaurant and escorted Lara to a table out on the terrace. Although they had missed the lunch hour and the kitchen was closed, Pierre always welcomed his afternoon clientele. He offered a romantic setting for intimate conversations mixed with expensive champagnes.

Lara looked radiant, her olive skin contrasting with her pink sundress. Her caramel-colored hair was swept away from her oval face and pulled up beneath a pink straw hat. Her almond-shaped dark eyes were gently shaded by the hat's full brim. Her teeth, like pearls, sparkled each time she smiled.

"Oh Markie," Lara said, transforming her laughter into a seductive smile, "your stories are so amusing! I'm so glad we finally got a chance to meet." She brought the tall crystal flute to her lips and slowly sipped the Dom Perignon. "Sal speaks highly of you, and I told her I was anxiously awaiting an introduction."

"I'm glad you were available at a minute's notice . . ." Markie refilled their glasses. "I don't get over to Walnut Creek that often."

Lara's tongue circled the thin rim of her glass, then dipped into the cool champagne. The liquid bubbled on the tip of her tongue, and she quickly pulled it back into her mouth.

"I've been warned that I should watch out for you . . . is that true?" Lara said. Her lips were the color of raspberries.

"Maybe," Markie responded. She grazed Lara's lips with her fingertip, following the thin, wet trail of warmth left by Lara's velvet tongue. "In fact," Markie continued in a sultry voice, "you can watch me as carefully as you want." Markie's fingertip had now explored the borders of Lara's soft lips and nudged the moist opening of her mouth.

"Is that so?" Lara whispered. She drew Markie's finger into her mouth with a simple sucking motion.

"Come on." Markie reached into her pocket and tossed a fifty-dollar bill on the table. She took Lara's hand. "I'm losing control."

Lara did not say a word as Markie led her from the veranda into the main dining area and then quietly through a side door that led into the restaurant's large empty kitchen.

Abruptly Markie turned to Lara, pushing her up against the long cooking counter in the center of the room, taking Lara into her arms and kissing her passionately on her strawberry lips.

A muffled moan escaped Lara's lips as she tried to speak. Markie was not giving her a chance to talk, continuing the full kisses on Lara's mouth as she lifted her up onto the table, tossing the straw hat aside.

"What . . ." Lara muttered between the kisses. "What if someone . . ."

"Dear Lara, the kitchen is closed. Pierre doesn't serve dinner on Sundays." Markie was pulling down the spaghetti straps on Lara's lacy pink sundress. "Didn't you tell Sal you wanted to play out a fantasy with a woman like me?" Markie whispered as she uncompromisingly swept her hands up Lara's smooth legs to the soft warm thighs and back down again.

"She told you that I said that?"

"And a fantasy with a woman like me entails risk, playing out on the edge." Markie continued to run her strong hands up under the pink dress. "Or is pretty Lara all talk?"

Markie slid her tongue down Lara's neck to her golden-hued shoulders, nipping the skin between her teeth. The flesh rose up in small welts as she bit her way down to the sundress where the curve of Lara's breast pressed the cotton and lace.

"Take me over the edge . . . any way you want it, Markie," Lara exclaimed. Markie felt shivers of ecstasy shoot through Lara's body.

As Markie unzipped the small zipper that ran down the back of Lara's dress, the bodice fell away to reveal Lara's rounded breasts. Her hardened nipples were large and dark as plums.

Markie immediately placed her face between the full breasts. She brushed her tongue, nose and hair against their perfume-dusted softness. Lara was moaning, her fingers tangled in Markie's hair.

Markie looked up at Lara. "You are so luscious," she said. She scanned the array of condiments placed at the end of the kitchen counter and was able to reach over and dip her fingers into an open container of cooking oil. She flicked her tongue across Lara's wine-purple nipples.

Skimming her tongue back and forth from nipple to nipple, Markie paused a moment to suck gently, then hurriedly moved to Lara's other nipple. She latched on, tugging roughly.

Coated in the oil, Markie's hand slid under the dress, up Lara's silky thigh. Still kissing and sucking the breasts, Markie dipped her hand again into the oil, slathering a palmful to the other thigh. She worked her way between Lara's marvelous legs, massaging generous amounts of oil up and down both thighs. Raising the dress, she ran her hands up toward the thick, full triangle of hair and back down to Lara's knees.

"My dress! My dress will stain," Lara said, trying to sit upright as the oil dripped from between her thighs.

"I'll buy you a hundred dresses, a thousand dresses," Markie murmured. She poured another handful of oil on Lara's legs, covering them, coating them, roughly pushing her hands up and down the slippery surfaces.

"A thousand dresses," Lara whispered. She closed her eyes, lying back on the table.

Although Lara's legs were spread fully, Markie was unable to see between the fur-covered lips that expertly guarded Lara's treasures. Markie grabbed a set of cooking tongs and greased their square tips with oil. Brushing the cool metal against Lara's leg, she inched the tongs toward their destination . . . Lara's tight-lipped private cache.

Reaching the fragrant thatch, Markie shimmied the tongs between Lara's ample lips, slowly parting them, so the purple clitoris jutted forward. Markie let out a low moan. She loved olive-skinned women, loved their magenta-tinted pussies.

Markie hesitated. She wanted a moment to relish the beautiful sight in front of her. Lara's face was tilted to the side, her white teeth lightly skimming her dark red lower lip. Oh yes, Lara was willing to play on the edge.

A nearby jar of blackberry jam caught Markie's attention. Markie twisted off the lid and sank her finger into the thick jelly.

"Do you like blackberry jam?" Markie asked. She smeared the sugary confection across Lara's mouth. Markie planted her lips on Lara's, smearing the violet-black jelly across Lara's face with her tongue.

"Yes, I love jam, I love jam . . ." Lara's words were muffled beneath Markie's kisses.

"Mmm," Markie dipped her fingers back into the jar. "Especially jam on a lovely lady's lips."

Markie painted more preserves on Lara's lips,

taking her fingers and smoothing the berries down Lara's neck to her eager breasts, palming Lara's large nipples.

Lara began unbuttoning Markie's shirt, pulling it open, exposing the firm breasts. Following the cue, Markie climbed onto the counter and pressed against Lara. Slowly at first, she began to move her upper body in small circles smearing the jam between Lara and herself.

Slippery, slick, her own nipples extended to points. Moving even faster, squishing the warm jam each time she rubbed those hard buttons against Lara's, Markie licked, then lapped the sweetness from around Lara's face.

"You are so very, very sweet!" Markie said as she situated herself on her knees between Lara's legs. She positioned Lara's legs, one on each side, over her shoulders.

She then scooped some of the jam from Lara's breasts and glazed it between the open lips of Lara's pussy. The color of the jam accentuated the hue of Lara's clitoris as though the colors had been selected by an artist.

With the tongs, Markie stretched Lara's thick lips apart then sunk her tongue down into the sugary treat. Fluttering her tongue, she slid the tongs down to Lara's plum-tinted slit. Carefully, Markie applied just enough pressure to sink the utensil an inch or so into Lara's yielding cunt.

"Ah . . ." Lara groaned in pleasure as Markie separated the tongs just a bit, then closed them. The smooth metal pushed up against a hidden hot spot in Lara's pussy, causing her to arch involuntarily. Markie opened the tongs once again, grazing that small patch of sensitive tissue. She shut them and released them as she tapped her tongue and lowered her entire mouth onto the sticky flesh-pocket, mouthing the entire clitoris and suckling its swollen purple pedestal.

"You like that? You like that, baby?" Markie's voice was husky.

She was pumping the pulpy clit with her jaw, applying more pressure as she did so. Lara grasped the edge of the counter, running her tongue around her candied mouth.

"Yes, Markie, oh, please baby please . . . Yes!" Lara cried as she shuddered into climax.

"That's right," Markie said softly as she watched Lara's rigid body arch up in pleasure and then gradually relax. She lowered herself directly on top of Lara, enclosing Lara in her arms.

Markie suddenly flashed on Ruby who, by that time was probably concerned as to Markie's whereabouts, wondering why she hadn't come home. Markie held Lara, drawing her closer, as if Lara were some sort of life preserver.

I will *never,* Markie thought defiantly, *not ever,* be played.

Chapter 23

Four o'clock had turned into four-thirty, four-thirty into five, and there was still no word from Markie. Ruby shot another glance at the telephone on the night stand. She had already left four messages on Markie's answering machine. There was no point in calling again.

Ruby shifted on her bed, covering her face with the rose-colored pillow. She felt absolutely horrid.

"Why, as a matter of fact, yes," Sal had said when Ruby telephoned her only moments ago, following the calls to the Highway Patrol and hospitals. "Markie *had* mentioned something about *unfinished business* in Walnut Creek . . ."

It was unlike Markie not to call, not to let Ruby know there had been a change, that she would be delayed. Pressing her face into the pillow, Ruby was overwhelmed by a sudden disconcerting feeling — something was happening, something damaging was occurring, and it wasn't Markie who would be the victim.

Reaching for her stuffed bear, Ruby clung to its furry body, struggled with the gnawing, empty sensation inside her heart. She was overreacting. Markie was probably trapped in a conversation with real-estate clients and was trying as politely as possible to slip away. Hadn't that scenario happened before? But in the past, Markie had called, *always* called, to let Ruby know.

There was something wrong. She just couldn't figure it out. Maybe it was Sal's smug "unfinished business" that held deeper implications.

The unexpected ring of the doorbell startled Ruby out of her troubled thoughts. "Markie!" she said aloud, feeling a mixture of anger and relief as she rushed to the front door.

"Hello, hello, sweet baby!" Markie, cradling an armful of flowers, gave Ruby a kiss on the cheek as she waltzed into the apartment, surrounded by an aura of self-assuredness.

"I am *so* sorry I couldn't call. I closed an important deal this afternoon. You know how those clients can be . . . but I feel good, great as a matter of fact! Like a burden's been lifted. And you and I are going to celebrate tonight!" Markie grabbed Ruby into her arms, letting the flowers fall to the floor.

"I was so worried. You didn't call . . ." Ruby said between the kisses.

"No," Markie whispered as though speaking to herself, as if intoxicated by other thoughts. She ran her fingers through Ruby's thick hair. Her words were barely audible. "No need for you to worry anymore."

Chapter 24

There's this theory — maybe it's Eastern philosophy — about following your intuition, your gut feeling, or whatever you want to call that little voice inside. But that night, when Markie showed up at my house overflowing with flowers and ready to celebrate, even though my internal antennae were up and beeping "trouble," I made a conscious choice to disregard the warning signals.

Don't try to make me believe someone else would have, *could* have, handled things differently! I swear to God, the way she grabbed me, sweet-talking me like there was nothing else in the world but her and me. Those tight jeans, the black silver-heeled boots she wore . . .

Part of me had been scared when Markie hadn't shown up or called. And sure, I had been angry. But Markie could be pretty convincing when she wanted to be — or maybe I should say, when I wanted so desperately to believe her.

Did I stop to question the fact she had worn jeans to a business meeting? Did I wonder what that interesting, unfamiliar perfume was that lightly scented her hair? No. Not at that moment. And later, when those persistent doubts kept haunting me, I did my best to find logical answers. The jeans? Markie must have gone home to change before showing up at my house. The new exotic perfume? She had, quite simply, used a new shampoo. Whatever the doubt, I produced a simple explanation.

I was able to rationalize that first incident. But over the next few weeks, Markie's attitude began to change. There was a certain edge, a deliberate cockiness in her voice. She would make dates with me and show up late. She would promise to call and then be "too busy" to get to a phone. Her business deals were taking up more and more of her time.

But the night finally arrived when she pushed me too far. We were at McCarthy's Bar and Grill, maybe three weeks later. I had been harboring the nagging fear that I was losing Markie, but I wasn't willing to share this ugly secret with her. After all, every shrewd woman knows that the best way to drive a lover away is to start clinging. I tried to dispel those worries, half-heartedly convincing myself that I was premenstrual and clearly the victim of a hormonal reality void.

In the middle of dinner, she excused herself — a habit she had recently developed, saying she needed to use the restroom. Out of the blue, I decided to follow her — just in time to make the disconcerting discovery that her destination was the telephone, not the restroom. And there she stood — laughing seductively into the phone. Oh yes, I recognized that laugh.

A horrible sinking sensation raced through me. I wanted to run to the restroom, lean over the toilet, vomit up all the sickness I suddenly felt. Instead, slightly dizzy and disoriented, I found my way back to the booth.

I dipped my napkin into my water glass and wiped its coolness across my forehead, watching Markie as she sauntered back to the booth, a smile on her face. That smile, that cocky expression, was more than I could tolerate!

"What the hell is going on!" I snapped as Markie reached the table.

Markie turned, looking over her shoulder, as if I were possibly talking to someone behind her. She shot a glance back to me and slid into the booth.

"What are you going off about, Rube?" Markie said with a bewildered expression on her face.

"Is that it? Huh? Every single goddamned time you use the fucking restroom in a restaurant, is that what you're doing? Calling your goddamned lover?" I was trembling, out of control, trying to hold in all the anxiety I had felt the last few weeks.

"My lover?" Markie had lowered her voice,

perhaps in an attempt to persuade me to follow suit. "What in heaven's name are you talking about? I made a simple business call and you —"

"A business call? A *simple* business call! Is that what you want me to believe? I saw you! I heard you! I recognize 'sweet-talking' Markie playing her game!"

"You heard the conversation? Or are you making all kinds of unfounded accusations, based on . . ." Markie paused, taking a moment to think. ". . . based on the fact that it's three days before your period?"

"Don't you dare give me that shit!" I said furiously, wanting to rid myself of all the anger pent up inside me. The hours of being taken for granted! The days of thinking I was no longer important enough! The weeks of feeling abandoned, of having been so frightened, wondering if I was losing her. I had not wanted to push her even further away with jealousy and insecurity and I had tried like a dog to appear loving and understanding.

"Where have you been, Markie, the last few weeks? Who the hell are you anymore?" I tossed my napkin on the table and left the restaurant.

I flagged down a cab, climbed into the back seat, and we raced off into the night. But to where? To goddamned where? I couldn't go home. There was no place I wanted to be without Markie.

"Or are you making all kinds of unfounded accusations?" she had said, that perplexed expression on her face. Well, were they unfounded?

At the Flowers Bar, sitting by myself, I stared at my reflection in the mirror. I sipped a brandy, trying to think things through. When I had first seen

Markie talking on the phone, I couldn't contain my feelings. Was it another woman? Was that why Markie had been acting so different lately?

Or had I been overreacting? Had Markie's behavior this last month *really* been out of the ordinary? She had been busy with her career lately, that was all. And here I was having a tantrum because I wasn't getting enough attention. God, what an incredible jerk I had been!

I glanced at my watch. It was two hours since I had dramatically left McCarthy's. Markie had probably first gone to my house, and then, despondently, on to her own. She was, most likely, sick with grief over the way I had accused her, not even giving her a chance to defend herself.

Placing five dollars on the bar, I took a final sip of the warm brandy and headed out to the street to catch a cab. I had no alternative but to get to Markie — my dear, sweet Markie — as soon as possible.

Chapter 25

Markie's house was dark when the taxi pulled up in front.

"Wait for me just a moment," Ruby said, handing the driver a ten-dollar bill. She climbed out of the cab, walked over to the garage and peered into the window. The car was there. Markie was home.

Ruby waved the cabbie on, then proceeded to the front door. She tapped lightly. No answer. Probably already in bed, Ruby thought. She fumbled in her purse for her key chain with the miniature flashlight attached to it.

Following the thin stream of light, Ruby carefully approached the back porch, the potted plant, the spare key. Within moments, she was inside Markie's kitchen.

Ruby hesitated, deliberating one last time the things she wanted to say to Markie. She was sorry for her anger, her childish behavior in the restaurant. She had been wrong in accusing, and even worse, assuming that Markie had taken another lover . . .

Her thoughts were interrupted by the sounds of faint moaning down the hall. She imagined Markie crying into her pillow, with nothing but the night to comfort her. An overpowering sensation of love, interwoven with remorse, engulfed Ruby.

How could she have doubted Markie? Warm memories flashed through Ruby's mind: Markie, in Ruby's apartment, her arms laden with flowers . . . Markie, in the restaurant, trailing perfume across Ruby's breasts . . . Markie, giving her the ring . . . Markie kissing her, Markie holding her.

Ruby clicked on the penlight and tiptoed down the darkened hallway to Markie's room. Wanting only to get to Markie, to make things right again, Ruby quickly opened the bedroom door.

"Oh Markie, I've been such a fool!" Ruby said apologetically, her eyes adjusting to the dim candlelight that surrounded Markie's bed like a golden canopy.

It was in that moment, that horrible, horrible moment, that Markie — seemingly in slow motion — pulled herself up from between Lara's long legs.

"Oh Jesus," Lara muttered, covering her breasts with a pillow.

Markie grabbed her robe and climbed out of bed. "Ruby, this isn't what you think —"

"Isn't what I think! Isn't what I think? Tell me it's a business deal! Tell me it's a goddamned business deal and I'll spit in your face!" Ruby hissed, unable to pull herself away yet wanting desperately to get out. She was immobilized, her legs like lead.

"We need to talk," Markie said, her voice calm. She touched Ruby's arm.

Ruby pushed Markie away, turned, and rushed down the hall.

"Look, Ruby," Markie said as she reached the living room where Ruby, sobbing, had collapsed against the front door. "I didn't mean to hurt you. It's just that things didn't work out between us."

Markie's words pierced Ruby's heart like poisoned darts. Ruby was stunned. She could barely breathe.

"What the hell are you saying to me? What the hell are you saying to me!" Ruby yelled. "Since when wasn't it working out? Why haven't I been told about this sudden turn of events?" Ruby's heart was pounding. She pushed herself away from the door and glared at Markie. "What are you saying to me!"

"Obviously," Markie said flatly, "we both have been exploring our feelings the last few months and —"

Ruby, hearing the lack of emotion in Markie's voice, flew out of control. She began slapping wildly at Markie. Sobbing, she screamed, "Who the fuck are you? A soulless monster?"

"My dear Ruby," Markie said, grabbing Ruby's arms. "I am no different than you are. We played the game — a game, as you well know, where there's always a winner and always a loser. Unfortunately, this time, *you're* the loser. You can comprehend that concept, can't you?"

The room filled with a deafening silence. Ruby couldn't move. Her body, racked with pain, felt as though she had been repeatedly stabbed. The walls seemed splattered with the blood of her love.

Ruby couldn't believe the words she had just heard. An incredible anger began to swell in her. Ruby filled her mouth with saliva, pooled every bit of brute force within herself, and spit directly into Markie's face. She pushed Markie away and slammed out the front door and into the cool night air.

Chapter 26

Markie closed the front door and sighed. It was most unfortunate that things had to end so nastily, but who would have guessed that Ruby would brazenly sneak into her home, into her bedroom, and make a scene in front of Lara? And if Markie had not handled the situation properly, had not been tough with Ruby, Lara would have had the ammunition to show Markie as a henpecked woman.

It was just as well, Markie thought. She had seen the whole thing coming, the break-up and all. Women in the community had started talking — or so Sal had confided — implying that Markie had finally been broken, had been taken in under Ruby's spell. And over the past few weeks, when she was out on the town, Markie could sense women looking at her, whispering about her. She really had no choice but to end the relationship before it ruined her reputation.

Sure, she had almost gotten too involved with Ruby, and had decided at that point to wind things down, to not see Ruby as often, to not be quite as attentive, to take on a new lover. Eventually, word would get around that Markie had grown bored with Ruby. Another star for Markie's status as a player, and that would be that.

Ruby had gone too far. The unexpected visit, the confrontation in front of Lara — Ruby had acted as if she controlled Markie! The harsh words, the hitting . . . Markie had had no alternative but to get unpleasant, to salvage her reputation before Lara had a chance to say Markie had been pussy-whipped! It had been necessary for Markie to say what she had to Ruby, to play it as though this "affair" with Ruby had been no big deal.

After what Lara had heard that night, and if Markie knew Lara like she thought she did, by tomorrow everyone in the community would be, once again, looking up to Markie, the hottest woman in town.

Chapter 27

Ruby raced out of Markie's house and ran blindly down the street, tears streaming her face. A constant aching sensation pulsated through her body. She wanted only to get away, as fast as possible, from the icy coldness in Markie's blank eyes.

What had happened? What in God's name could have happened? Why hadn't she followed her intuition? All that time she had spent worrying the last few weeks, talking herself out of what she knew deep down to be the truth, Markie had been betraying her. Ruby remembered everything Candace had said to her so many months before. Could all those stories and rumors have been valid?

Ruby had been played for a fool! Played for a goddamned fool!

Ruby slowed her pace, taking a long moment to catch her breath. Who the fuck did Markie think she was? What had Markie said? That they were players . . . and Ruby had lost? Well, Ruby knew how to take care of herself! She didn't need Markie. There were plenty of women who would be more than happy to take Markie's place!

She would telephone a cab, return to the Flowers Bar, and within an hour, Ruby would be in another woman's arms. Markie would be a fading memory.

Chapter 28

I glanced across the bar to the blonde. The woman was hot all right, with her spiked hair, her black leather jacket. Just my type. I could feel her checking me out too. I caught a brief glimpse of my reflection in the mirror. Okay, I admit it, I looked a little ragged. After all, I had been crying for the last half hour. But I had enough attitude, I had enough goddamned attitude to bring any woman to her knees. And the blonde . . . she was leaning up against the bar. I wanted the blonde and I was going to have her.

So I had gotten off track with Markie. Big deal. I was going to be just fine. I needed a distraction, that was all.

The blonde, sporting the most seductive smile I had seen in a good long time, looked me straight in the eye. And believe me, the smile I returned left no questions about my intentions. I sipped my vodka, ran my hand nonchalantly through my thick hair. I had a pretty face, smooth skin, naturally curly hair, a well-proportioned, size-six body. Who wouldn't want to see how hot I could be? She wouldn't resist. I was an expert at this game, one of the very best. Ask anyone and you'd find out quick enough my standing in the community.

The blonde pushed away from the bar and walked over to where I was seated. I let out a low sigh. The best medicine for a blow like the one Markie had delivered was heading right toward me. Thank God I knew how to tend my own wounds!

I could see her reflection in the mirror as she moved behind me, leaning toward me.

"Penetrating," she said, her voice was deep, sultry.

I turned to face her.

"Your eyes . . ." She traced the corner of my eye with her finger. "I could feel you burning into me."

She was only inches away. She wore a tempting blend of gardenias and cloves that perfumed us both. Amethyst earrings matched the color of her eyes.

"You felt me from across the room, did you?" I sugar-coated my femme voice. "And what else, if I may be so bold to ask, did you feel?"

She moved closer to me. The rich scent of leather, the rustle of her jacket, added even more to her allure. She grabbed a handful of my hair and jerked my face toward her full lips. "My bike's outside, and that's *exactly* where you want to be. Right?"

I nodded. I had a sudden vision of climbing onto her Harley, cutting into the night, escaping Markie.

She took my hand, led me out of the Flowers Bar to the back parking lot to her motorcycle, and climbed on, motioning for me to follow.

"My name is Loren," she said.

I straddled the bike, reaching around her as the power of the starting engine vibrated through me.

"Ruby."

"Ruby. That's my birthstone," she said as the bike started to roll. "The gem of passion."

"Yes, passion." I held her tightly as we pushed into the night on her black-and-silver stallion.

Chapter 29

They crisscrossed the city, to the Golden Gate Bridge and into Marin County. Ruby, clutching Loren, felt weighted down. It was almost as if the ghost of Markie had been waiting patiently for her in the Flowers Bar parking lot. Taking advantage of Ruby's momentary distraction, it had climbed aboard the motorcycle and clung tenaciously to Ruby's back.

Her eyes clenched, Ruby pressed closer against Loren. Get off! Leave me alone! she demanded silently, trying hopelessly to shake the uninvited apparition.

As the motorcycle slowed, Ruby opened her eyes. They had pulled up to the edge of a cliff overlooking the bay. The city sparkled in the distance like a diamond broach.

"No one seems to know about this place," Loren said. "Every time I've ever been here, it's always been deserted."

Burdened by the albatross on her back, Ruby slid off the bike. Please, she pleaded silently as Loren wrapped her arms around her, please help me break the spell.

Loren carried Ruby across the dirt road and laid her down on a large grassy area. They looked out beyond the edge of the cliff to the shimmering city lights.

"A ruby to complete the tiara," Loren said as she lay on top of Ruby.

Ruby reached up for the blonde butch, bringing Loren's cool lips to her own. A feeling of desperation swept through her. I must rid myself of Markie, she thought. I must! I must! She grabbed Loren, kissed her, bit her and muttered, "Please! please have me now. Have me now!"

Loren yanked off Ruby's jacket, ripped her blouse and began to suck recklessly on Ruby's hard nipples.

"Yes, Loren, yes!" Ruby moaned, arching up her full breasts. "Now put your fingers in me," she demanded. "Hurry! Put your fingers in me! Take me, goddamn you. Take me!"

Loren grabbed at Ruby's pants, pulled them down

to her ankles, and rammed her thick fingers into Ruby's dampness.

"Yes! Harder! Harder! Break the spell! Break the spell!"

Loren plunged her fingers over and over into the soft heat of Ruby's pussy. "You're hot, baby," Loren grunted.

"Please!" Ruby screamed at the image of Markie that haunted her. "Get the hell away! Get the hell away from me!" Pushing, she fought to break the spell.

"Jesus, lady!" Loren said, pulling back. "What do you want? Should I fuck you or get the hell away?"

"I don't fuck!" Ruby said as she broke down into a sea of tears. "I don't fuck!" She was crying uncontrollably.

"God! I'm sorry, Ruby. You told me to take you, to have you, to put my fingers in you . . ."

"I . . . I . . ." Ruby tried to speak between the sobbing.

"What is it, Ruby? Can I help you?"

"No." Ruby took a deep breath, struggling to calm herself. She peered out at the distant city. The lights blurred through her veil of her tears. "There's nothing you can do. Nothing anyone can do." She wiped her eyes and watched as the blear of lights seemed to gel into a brilliant necklace strung cross San Francisco.

Staring out at the city, Ruby was struck with the horrible realization that having another woman was not going to stop the hurt, was not going to help her escape. The cure-all she had relied on for so many years no longer worked. She was trapped — all alone — with the incredible pain of what Markie had done to her.

Ruby covered her face with her hands, aware of a trembling sensation deep within her soul. Suddenly she was terrified.

Chapter 30

Ruby unlocked her front door and gave a limp wave to Loren, who nodded, revved the motorcycle, and sped off into the night. Stepping into the apartment, Ruby felt an alarming emptiness. She glanced around the living room. It was odd, she had almost expected to enter her home and find it vandalized — her most valued possessions indiscriminately scattered about, rummaged through, tossed aside. Yet everything stood as it had when she left.

"It's just me now," Ruby said aloud, tossing her

jacket on the couch, walking distractedly toward her bedroom. She thought of the last hallway she had walked down, the last bedroom she had walked into, seeing Markie in bed with some stranger, Markie saying "This isn't what you think." And what could she have possibly meant? What explanation could Markie have possibly given?

The answering machine was blinking — one call. Ruby hurried to the nightstand. Had Markie called? Perhaps this had been a misunderstanding of the largest magnitude. Perhaps there was a reasonable explanation . . .

Ruby pushed the message button, her heart pounding.

A click and a dial tone. The person had hung up. Markie must have tried to call, of course. Markie most certainly had called. Ruby had been wild, out of herself, when she had found Markie with that woman. And Markie, taken off guard, had said things without thinking, to protect herself.

Ruby pulled a sheet of her finest stationery from the lavender box on her desk. She took an envelope and quickly scribbled Markie's name across it.

I need to write her a note, to tell her that I'm willing to give her a chance to explain herself, Ruby thought. She sprayed the sheet of stationery with a considerable amount of *Jouer* perfume.

MARKIE —

HOW COULD YOU HAVE *EVER EVER* DONE THIS TO ME?

I AM PRAYING THAT SOMEHOW A MISTAKE

Ruby's writing was interrupted by the shrill ring of the telephone. "Markie!" she whispered. Her heartbeat quickened. She stared at the phone. She did not want to pick up the receiver until Markie left her sorrowful explanation on Ruby's answering machine.

"Hello Ruby. This is me, Carmen. I know we haven't been in contact, but I heard the news tonight, and I thought you might be needing a friend."

Heard the news! Heard the news! Ruby thought, filled with immediate rage. *Who* had already spread the news? It hadn't even been three hours since she had rushed out of Markie's house. Cruel and heartless, Markie had betrayed Ruby even further.

"No! No! No!" Ruby cried. She grabbed her stuffed bear and clung to it.

The aching inside her was more than she could take. How could she have fantasized a reconciliation with Markie? Markie had taken another woman to her bed. With an icy glare, Markie had spoken of winners and losers, as if their relationship had been a game. She had played Ruby for a fool. Evidently, Markie already was out on the town and boasting of her conquest. Ruby could visualize the new woman hanging on Markie's arm, like a trophy.

"Oh God!" Ruby moaned, crawling out of bed. Dizzy, she stumbled to the sink and covered her face with a shower of cool water. "I just can't stand it. I absolutely just can't stand it." She was sobbing, racking with pain. How deep the knife of the betrayal had plunged, slashing her, tearing her heart to shreds.

A sickening vision of women at the bar flashed into her mind. They were laughing, saying, "Poor,

poor Ruby. Another one of Markie's playthings cast aside."

How could she face any of them again! A plaything! Trapped in Markie's web! Up until that night, Ruby had been known as an enchantress, a woman not to be taken lightly . . . and now her reputation was ruined. Everyone would look at her and know.

Ruby leaned over the sink, shook her head, reached for a washcloth to dry her face. Who could respect her after this? The thought ricocheted in Ruby's mind and began to spiral down through her body. She felt a stirring so intense that she could barely breathe. She grabbed the edge of the sink, giving in to a sudden compulsion to look up into the mirror. And there, almost as if it had been waiting a lifetime for recognition, her own reflection stared back at her with haunted eyes.

Chapter 31

The first few weeks after Markie? What that was like for me? My reputation as a femme fatale was ruined, and I was forced to face the ugly realization that the only thing hot about me was the sordid details of the Markie-Ruby break-up.

To this day, I still remember how sick I felt after hearing Carmen's phone message. It had been only a few hours since I discovered Markie in bed with Lara, and after Carmen's call, there was no doubt that the news had already spread through the community. It's like this: if Carmen knew, then within an hour everyone knew.

I have an image of myself stumbling across the room, splashing water on my face, hoping to rouse myself out of the dreadful nightmare I had entered. I was all alone. There was no one who really cared about me anymore. Slowly, over the months, I had abandoned my friends one by one and replaced them with Markie. Now there was no Markie and no friends. The call from Carmen? I knew she called me for one reason only, to get the scoop.

So I stood at the sink that first night, just stared into the mirror, contemplating the woman who gazed back at me. The eyes held my attention. Sure, I'd looked at myself in the mirror. Let's face it, I've spent plenty of time in front of the mirror, but I had never felt what I felt that night, never seen that particular image.

I looked awful — pale, defeated, almost as if the bright, vibrant, exciting Ruby had been destroyed. Where had she gone? Who the hell was Ruby anyway?

I stayed in bed for several days, took a leave of absence from work, said I was sick. Yet I felt more than sick. I was dying. Isolated, I spent the hours alternately crying, screaming, and numbly staring into a small hand mirror. Stuck in timeless inertia, and eternal emptiness, washed in despair, I felt shattered, barely alive.

Then came the night of the dream. An intensely vivid dream that I'll never forget. I was on a journey, wandering deep into a cave. Alone, stripping off layer after layer of clothing, I descended further and further, away from my life as I knew it. Large gilt mirrors were surrounded by the golden glow of candlelight. I passed small alcoves where, in one, Markie was beckoning me to come to her. In others, I saw Jean crying, reaching for me, Lenny scattering flowers, whirling, Valerie seated before a table covered with jewelry. I started running. The cave seemed to get smaller, darker. The air was thin and I couldn't breathe. Suddenly, a blinding explosion blocked the pathway with a fiery display. I stood, stunned by the heat, watching the ball of flame as it first roared and then quickly extinguished, transforming itself into a mirror, the borders of which were still smoldering. I peered into the mirror, horrified to see that my face was decaying, the skin rotting off in layers. I covered my eyes and began to scream. I woke up covered in sweat.

I brought the hand mirror to my face, unsure of what was dream and what was reality, frightened of what I would now see. My face was still intact, but there was something different about my eyes. A dim sparkle, deep inside their darkness, transfixed me. It was almost as if I had connected to a pathway that led down into my soul.

At that moment, I saw myself clearly. Hot, provocative Ruby, always in the right clothes, always with a woman on her arm, always having a back-up woman waiting in the wings, never caring about the consequences, I was beginning to accept the slow destruction of what I thought was me and at the same time, I began to witness the rebirth of a new self.

Not that everything suddenly got better. But over the next few weeks, I became aware of a connection with my true self. I returned to work, read novels, took myself to movies, went on long walks. Still, I spent most of my time just sitting alone and crying. I was learning to open my heart to the pain instead of trying to mask it with a series of new lovers. Sure, I had "setback" days — days I was so unbearably lonely I'd end up driving out to Amanda's Bar and try to convince myself that taking a woman to bed would ease the pain. That old tried-and-true behavior always used to work in the past. But each time I made the moves, I could never go through with it. The thought of actually having someone in bed made me nauseous. I'd end up driving home alone instead.

But something good did surface from those drives to Amanda's, even if it wasn't quite what I had anticipated. I was sitting at the bar, checking out a redhead across the room, when I overheard a couple of women talking about a theater group that was starting at the Women's Center. I'm not sure why it struck me, but the idea of being involved in drama sounded intriguing. By the end of the week, I was a full-fledged member of the theater group. And that's where I made two wonderful discoveries . . .

Chapter 32

There was something about improvisational drama that brought me in touch with my inner self. Perhaps it was the introspection, the need to tap deep emotions, that uncovered the pathway for me.

I don't know why I felt drawn to the group, but I started attending once a week. We would split up into groups of two and do improvisation exercises with each other. Angela, the coach, described this technique as "processing."

We'd be given a situation and then have to create a scene with our partners in front of the rest of the women. We practiced this kind of exercise for a few weeks, and finally it was my turn.

Nanette and I were a team. We stood in front of the group as Angela gave us the scenario. I'm not sure if it was fate or what, but the one she chose for us was a classic. Nanette and I were supposed to be in a relationship and she was leaving me for another woman.

My first response was to clam up. The last thing I wanted to do was replay a scene like that! But Nanette started, and as she spoke to me — looking at me, speaking with downcast eyes and a nervous voice — I don't know what happened. Suddenly, I connected with the part. Before I had a chance to examine what I would say, I was pouring out feelings. I said everything I had wanted to say to Markie, but hadn't had the chance. I swear, when we were finished with our performance, the room filled with a stark silence. I looked up. The women were still, just staring at me.

An overwhelming urge came over me to rush out of the room. I had exposed my innermost emotions. This juicy episode would be broadcast through the entire women's community by evening . . . I had no doubts about that.

I felt dizzy, my face was damp from the tears that had not yet dried. I wanted to vomit.

Abruptly, the silence in the room broke as one, then two, and then finally all the women applauded. I turned to Nanette who had taken my hand in hers.

"To reveal one's soul through drama is a gift," Nanette said quietly. "Cherish it."

Chapter 33

After class, Susan approached Ruby and placed her hand on Ruby's shoulder. Ruby turned toward her.

"Ruby," Susan said shyly, "I just want to tell you that your performance today was riveting."

Ruby paused, appraising Susan's short dark hair, the tortoise-shell glasses. She knew Susan from the bars, but had never really spoken to her. In the past, they had traveled in different crowds, but occasionally they'd find themselves attending the same event. Not having much in common, they might have noticed each other from afar, but Ruby hadn't had much time for a woman like Susan.

Susan had known who Ruby was. Who didn't know who Ruby was? And although Ruby might have been every woman's fantasy, at least for a weekend tryst, Ruby was one of the "love them and leave them" players in the community, not someone Susan would have spent the time or energy pursuing.

But the untouchable persona of Ruby as Susan had always known her seemed to have disappeared. In a room full of strangers stood a different Ruby — a woman willing to reveal herself in front of everyone. Susan was aware of the rumors about the torrid romance and devastating breakup between Ruby and Markie. Who hadn't heard? Ruby was known as a master at the sport of breaking hearts. Who would have guessed she could have been hit so hard by her own game? And not only had she been hit, she had been willing to make it known, to expose a shattered self.

Susan looked Ruby in the eyes and completed her statement. "Really. I was impressed. We all were. I suppose you've been acting for a long time?"

Ruby took a long moment to think before she spoke, aware of the ambiguous nature of Susan's question. "Yes," Ruby responded honestly. "I've been acting for a *very* long time."

Chapter 34

If someone had told me six months before I went for coffee with Susan that she and I would end up in a relationship, I would have laughed at the improbability. Susan was a nurse who didn't impress the fast circle of women I used to hang out with. The idea of a relationship would have been ludicrous. But there I was, at a small cafe sitting across from Susan, and I was enchanted.

She talked about how hard it had been for her in her past relationships. She said she had an overwhelming tendency to try to save her lovers from their problems. Eventually, exhausted, she had realized the need to let go of her patterns. Her last lover had walked out on her, threatened and angered by this "new Susan." Susan had been devastated. Since then, she had been alone, doing in depth work on herself, joining the theater group.

She told me she was stunned by my ability to let go in the group. She had been working a long time to be able to say what hurt her, how she had tried to fix everyone else's problems.

As she spoke, I had a desire to share my loneliness and fears with her. My self image had also been shattered and, like Susan, I was struggling to come to terms with this "new Ruby."

It was the first time I'd wanted to confide these feelings. It was a strange concept. I had been a woman who thrived on risk taking, and I realized that when it came to the *real* risks in life, I had taken the easy way out. Not anymore. I wanted a second chance.

Without even thinking, I admitted to Susan how I had played women without concern for who got hurt, how I desperately went from lover to lover to avoid the possibility of being abandoned first, how I was afraid that if I revealed my neediness, no one would ever love me. Never opening my heart, getting out before it got too risky, too intimate, I had protected myself at any expense.

"You were so busy protecting yourself from abandonment that you brought that very end upon yourself, didn't you?" Susan said, taking my hand in hers.

"Yes," I murmured, teary-eyed. "I did."

Chapter 35

They had sat in the cafe for almost three hours when Susan asked Ruby to come to her home, to hold her through the night. Lying next to each other, Ruby was aware of how right it felt. A certain tranquility surrounded them as Susan, the sweet scent of honeysuckle in her hair, enclosed Ruby in her arms, kissing her over and over, their tongues gently touching as they luxuriated in holding each other.

"I feel so close to you," Ruby whispered into

Susan's ear. "Before, I never felt I was in a place that I belonged."

"Yes, lovely Ruby," Susan said, softly caressing Ruby's breast. "It's the same for me."

A wave of peacefulness passed through Ruby as Susan's fingers lightly glided across her breasts. For the first time, Ruby did not feel that she needed to be sexual to ensure Susan's interest in her. Instead, she had a deep desire to express the bond she felt with Susan.

"I want to make love with you," Ruby said, surprised by her own nervousness. She was on a new frontier, in bed with a woman because she wanted to share love with her, not because she needed to use sex to win love.

Ruby wasn't quite sure what making love in this way entailed. She didn't feel the need to pretend or masquerade as a femme fatale. She just wanted to touch and be touched.

Susan, as if sensing the newness of the situation, turned to Ruby. "Listen," she said as she ran her fingers across Ruby's forehead. "I want to make love with you, too, but I'm scared, scared I'll want you too much, scared you'll run away."

"I'm afraid, too. What if you see who I am and not like me? What if you don't want to see me after tonight? How could I cope with being abandoned again? But you know what, Susan? I can take care of myself, whether you walk out or not. And that knowledge, knowing that I fill the empty place in my heart, not you or anyone else — makes it okay to take the risk. I can open my heart, because no matter what you choose to do, I'll survive. Making love to you, opening up to you — I'm willing to take that risk."

Susan sighed. "Yes. A risk."

Ruby took Susan in a tender embrace, kissing and nibbling on Susan's scented neck. As if she were unveiling a porcelain doll, Ruby slowly lowered the sheet to reveal Susan's large pale breasts frosted with rosy pink tips.

Ruby took the full aureole into her mouth, creating enough suction to cause the nipple to stiffen into a perfect, square-shaped bud.

Ruby flicked her tongue lightly down to Susan's rounded belly, pausing at the pinched crevice of her belly button. Ruby's tongue darted in and out while her hands continued to Susan's angora-covered pussy. Parting the lips, Ruby slid her finger up and down the slick flesh.

Susan closed her eyes and listened as Ruby whispered, "How very lovely, how very sweet."

Ruby sensed a stirring, almost a heated tingling, beginning between Susan's moistened lips that protected her vagina.

Ruby rolled over, pulling Susan above her. "Straddle me, let me taste you."

As Susan spread herself above Ruby's face, Ruby guided Susan onto her anxiously awaiting tongue. Searching for the clitoris, Ruby pressed her tongue back and forth trying to locate it.

"Tell me how to please you, Susan," Ruby murmured, lapping the flowerlike flesh.

"I don't know . . . I never have an easy time. It's always a real task to find the exact spot."

"Is that so?" Ruby said. She was already aroused, and this challenge excited her even more.

She grabbed Susan's ass and began easily, deliberately, to suck Susan's pink mass of clitoral skin. She pulled the entire mound into her mouth as if she were a newborn baby latching onto its mother's breast. Hungrily Ruby milked it, not caring if she couldn't find the clit directly, only aware that Susan was beginning to grind her hips down against her mouth.

Pumping on the meaty flap, without regard for anything except for the intense need to draw the tissue deeper into her mouth, Ruby kneaded it between her tongue and palate. She was intoxicated by the taste, her face saturated with the exotic blend of Susan's tart sweetness.

Ruby reached up and tugged Susan's nipples while she continued to suck the swollen pussy.

Susan rotated her hips even faster. She grabbed the headboard and cried out in pleasure. Her back arched as she trembled into an overpowering orgasm.

Motionless, she stayed on top of Ruby for a moment, then collapsed, crying, into Ruby's arms. "Oh Ruby, I'm so frightened." Susan was shaking, her tears falling like salty raindrops onto Ruby's cheek.

Dear God, Ruby thought, wrapping her arms tightly around Susan, pulling her as close as possible, wishing that she could somehow latch onto her. Ruby was frightened too.

Chapter 36

I'm not going to say things were easy or that Susan and I lived happily ever after, because I swear to God, we've had to work like hell to keep from falling apart.

And even though I had undergone a major emotional transformation after my relationship with Markie ended — and I felt more connected with myself and less dependent on searching for a backup lover — there were times when an undeniable urge would intensify and I'd find myself fantasizing about someone new to fill the emptiness inside.

Susan took the time to talk with me when something triggered my emotions. And lately, she says she can even recognize what she calls the "Ruby wants out" look. It's been difficult for us both, but even so, we've stuck it out. And tonight, we're celebrating our year-and-a-half anniversary!

Susan's been out of town all week visiting her family in Texas. We've never really spent this much time apart. At first, I admit I was haunted by the old feelings — feelings I had thought were pretty much under control. I worried that once Susan had time away from me, she'd decide that she was much happier without dealing with me and all my bullshit. Maybe she'd even meet someone she thought was better than me. God! I could end up terribly hurt.

That's precisely the kind of thinking that causes me to lose my inner balance. I start to think I've become too dependent on Susan and that the only way out is to find a new woman. But one thing I *have* learned is that I have a choice.

So instead of stopping by the Flowers Bar for a drink the night Susan left, I ended up on a major shopping spree. And since then, I'm pretty sure I've defeated those demons from my past. Instead of obsessing about some new woman, I've spent the lonely nights talking into this tape recorder.

Actually, I'm glad the way things worked out this week with Susan out of town. Finding that letter to Markie gave me the time to sort through all those buried feelings and put them into proper perspective, once and for all.

Although, now that I've gone over the whole scenario, I can't seem to get my mind off Markie. Markie *must* have loved me. It was in her eyes, her voice. Maybe there were things she wanted to say to me but didn't know how? Maybe she still misses me. Perhaps I should call her — to say hello, to give her the chance to make amends. How could she *not* want to see me too?

Did I say "see me *too*?" You can't possibly think I was implying that I'd want to see Markie again. After all I've been through? All I've learned? I was reminiscing, that's all. I found the letter, read it, took the time to think things over . . . to get it out of my system. I promised myself when I began this retrospection: no romantic illusions, no obsessing. After all, that's exactly how I end up in trouble!

Chapter 37

Ruby peered into the mirror. The black pants looked hot, no doubt about it. And the boots! There really had been no choice but to buy them. They made the outfit. The shopping spree last Wednesday had been an overwhelming success. She looked good, very good, despite the bitter emptiness inside of her.

Markie. She missed Markie.

She had been an expert at denying those feelings for all those months! Markie, her first real love, at this very moment, was probably thinking of her.

Ruby's obsessing was momentarily distracted by

the doorbell. Susan. It was their anniversary night, and Ruby had spent the last few hours missing — no, more than missing — she was craving Markie. It was an ugly realization.

Ruby opened the door. Susan was smiling, her arms filled with a bouquet of flowers and a package wrapped in ice-blue paper.

"Sweetie!" Susan tossed the flowers and the gift on the couch, pulling Ruby into her arms. "God, you look absolutely gorgeous. I've missed you so much!" Susan began sprinkling kisses across Ruby's lips.

"I've missed you, too," Ruby said, trying to sound as if all was well, as if nothing had changed. She was not ready to admit to herself, let alone to Susan, that she was tangled in her own web.

"Rube, what is it?" Susan said, aware of the distraction in Ruby's voice.

Ruby, suddenly feeling smothered, wanted to scream. Must she share everything with Susan?

"You've closed down, haven't you?" Susan stared at Ruby, as if recognizing that tell-tale look on Ruby's face. She glanced around the room, noticing the tape machine, the thin piece of stationery resting on top of it.

"What's all this, Ruby?" She walked to the table and picked up the letter.

"I went shopping," Ruby said vaguely. "A major shopping spree and . . . I was trying to clean out my closet. I took a pile of things I don't wear anymore out to the garage. That's when I found the letter. I didn't mean for it to cause me so much . . . I didn't realize that it would —"

Susan took Ruby's hand and led her down the hall to the bedroom. Standing in front of the closet, she opened the door. The closet was still crammed with clothes.

"Not too successful at weeding out the old clothes, I see," Susan said, putting her arm around Ruby. "Fortunately, you have a woman like me to help you sort through this stuff. Like these jeans, this blouse. You haven't worn them once since I've known you."

Ruby stood there, quiet.

"Do you *really* need them, or are you just frightened of the empty place after they're gone?" Susan said softly, "Listen Ruby, I'm not going to leave you. And I truly believe that after all you've been through, you could never really abandon yourself either."

"God! Susan, I'm so sorry," Ruby said. Her restrained emotions began to avalanche into grief. "I *hate* this. I thought I was so together, so on top of things . . . only to find out how vulnerable, how weak, I actually am. Won't this ever end?"

Why, Ruby thought as a tear fell across her cheek, after all the changes I've made since Markie, all the soul-searching, am I still struggling with the same demons?

She could rid herself of Susan and these problems so easily with one call to Markie. Part of her wanted to make that call that instant. To get out, to find safety in the newness of yet another relationship — it could be so easy. Ruby tried to fantasize the attention, the wining and the dining.

But then what? How would she protect herself against Markie abandoning her? Take a lover on the side? And then another and then another? The idea was suddenly exhausting.

"This is your struggle," Susan whispered, as if

remembering her own work in therapy. She paused to collect her thoughts, as if remembering *her* pattern of trying to save her lovers. "Let the struggle feed your inner power, *not* your weakness."

The struggle *was* a symbol of inner power. Ruby considered Susan's words. Abandoning oneself is war, Ruby thought, certain she would *not* be calling Markie. She let out a long sigh, knowing she had won her latest battle.

Ruby relaxed as a fulfilling sense of peace passed through her. How far, indeed, in this journey she had come!

Ruby turned toward Susan, who had tears in her own eyes. Ruby was struck by the depth of Susan's love, Susan's understanding. She leaned over, brushing her lips across Susan's cheek, blotting the tears. Ruby then looked at the closet. Her new clothes *were* cramped, packed tightly next to the old. She was looking forward to having the much-needed space.

A CERTAIN DISCONTENT by Cleve Boutell. 240 pp. A unique coterie of women. ISBN 1-56280-009-4 9.95

GRASSY FLATS by Penny Hayes. 256 pp. Lesbian romance in the '30s. ISBN 1-56280-010-8 9.95

A SINGULAR SPY by Amanda K. Williams. 192 pp. 3rd spy novel featuring Lesbian agent Madison McGuire. ISBN 1-56280-008-6 8.95

THE END OF APRIL by Penny Sumner. 240 pp. A Victoria Cross Mystery. First in a series. ISBN 1-56280-007-8 8.95

A FLIGHT OF ANGELS by Sarah Aldridge. 240 pp. Romance set at the National Gallery of Art ISBN 1-56280-001-9 9.95

HOUSTON TOWN by Deborah Powell. 208 pp. A Hollis Carpenter mystery. Second in a series. ISBN 1-56280-006-X 8.95

KISS AND TELL by Robbi Sommers. 192 pp. Scorching stories by the author of *Pleasures.* ISBN 1-56280-005-1 9.95

STILL WATERS by Pat Welch. 208 pp. Second in the Helen Black mystery series. ISBN 0-941483-97-5 8.95

MURDER IS GERMANE by Karen Saum. 224 pp. The 2nd Brigid Donovan mystery. ISBN 0-941483-98-3 8.95

TO LOVE AGAIN by Evelyn Kennedy. 208 pp. Wildly romantic love story. ISBN 0-941483-85-1 9.95

IN THE GAME by Nikki Baker. 192 pp. A Virginia Kelly mystery. First in a series. ISBN 01-56280-004-3 8.95

AVALON by Mary Jane Jones. 256 pp. A Lesbian Arthurian romance. ISBN 0-941483-96-7 9.95

STRANDED by Camarin Grae. 320 pp. Entertaining, riveting adventure. ISBN 0-941483-99-1 9.95

THE DAUGHTERS OF ARTEMIS by Lauren Wright Douglas. 240 pp. Third Caitlin Reece mystery. ISBN 0-941483-95-9 8.95

CLEARWATER by Catherine Ennis. 176 pp. Romantic secrets of a small Louisiana town. ISBN 0-941483-65-7 8.95

THE HALLELUJAH MURDERS by Dorothy Tell. 176 pp. Second Poppy Dillworth mystery. ISBN 0-941483-88-6 8.95

ZETA BASE by Judith Alguire. 208 pp. Lesbian triangle on a future Earth. ISBN 0-941483-94-0 9.95

SECOND CHANCE by Jackie Calhoun. 256 pp. Contemporary Lesbian lives and loves. ISBN 0-941483-93-2 9.95

MURDER BY TRADITION by Katherine V. Forrest. 288 pp. A Kate Delafield Mystery. 4th in a series. ISBN 0-941483-89-4 18.95

BENEDICTION by Diane Salvatore. 272 pp. Striking, contemporary romantic novel. ISBN 0-941483-90-8 9.95

CALLING RAIN by Karen Marie Christa Minns. 240 pp. Spellbinding, erotic love story ISBN 0-941483-87-8 9.95

BLACK IRIS by Jeane Harris. 192 pp. Caroline's hidden past . . .
ISBN 0-941483-68-1 8.95

TOUCHWOOD by Karin Kallmaker. 240 pp. Loving, May/
December romance. ISBN 0-941483-76-2 8.95

BAYOU CITY SECRETS by Deborah Powell. 224 pp. A Hollis
Carpenter mystery. First in a series. ISBN 0-941483-91-6 8.95

COP OUT by Claire McNab. 208 pp. 4th Det. Insp. Carol Ashton
mystery. ISBN 0-941483-84-3 9.95

LODESTAR by Phyllis Horn. 224 pp. Romantic, fast-moving
adventure. ISBN 0-941483-83-5 8.95

THE BEVERLY MALIBU by Katherine V. Forrest. 288 pp. A
Kate Delafield Mystery. 3rd in a series. (HC) ISBN 0-941483-47-9 16.95
Paperback ISBN 0-941483-48-7 9.95

THAT OLD STUDEBAKER by Lee Lynch. 272 pp. Andy's affair
with Regina and her attachment to her beloved car.
ISBN 0-941483-82-7 9.95

PASSION'S LEGACY by Lori Paige. 224 pp. Sarah is swept into
the arms of Augusta Pym in this delightful historical romance.
ISBN 0-941483-81-9 8.95

THE PROVIDENCE FILE by Amanda Kyle Williams. 256 pp.
Second espionage thriller featuring lesbian agent Madison McGuire
ISBN 0-941483-92-4 8.95

I LEFT MY HEART by Jaye Maiman. 320 pp. A Robin Miller
Mystery. First in a series. ISBN 0-941483-72-X 9.95

THE PRICE OF SALT by Patricia Highsmith (writing as Claire
Morgan). 288 pp. Classic lesbian novel, first issued in 1952 . . .
acknowledged by its author under her own, very famous, name.
ISBN 1-56280-003-5 8.95

SIDE BY SIDE by Isabel Miller. 256 pp. From beloved author of
Patience and Sarah. ISBN 0-941483-77-0 9.95

SOUTHBOUND by Sheila Ortiz Taylor. 240 pp. Hilarious sequel
to *Faultline.* ISBN 0-941483-78-9 8.95

STAYING POWER: LONG TERM LESBIAN COUPLES
by Susan E. Johnson. 352 pp. Joys of coupledom.
ISBN 0-941-483-75-4 12.95

SLICK by Camarin Grae. 304 pp. Exotic, erotic adventure.
ISBN 0-941483-74-6 9.95

NINTH LIFE by Lauren Wright Douglas. 256 pp. A Caitlin
Reece mystery. 2nd in a series. ISBN 0-941483-50-9 8.95

PLAYERS by Robbi Sommers. 192 pp. Sizzling, erotic novel.
ISBN 0-941483-73-8 9.95

MURDER AT RED ROOK RANCH by Dorothy Tell. 224 pp.
First Poppy Dillworth adventure. ISBN 0-941483-80-0 8.95

LESBIAN SURVIVAL MANUAL by Rhonda Dicksion.
112 pp. Cartoons! ISBN 0-941483-71-1 8.95

A ROOM FULL OF WOMEN by Elisabeth Nonas. 256 pp.
Contemporary Lesbian lives. ISBN 0-941483-69-X 8.95

MURDER IS RELATIVE by Karen Saum. 256 pp. The first
Brigid Donovan mystery. ISBN 0-941483-70-3 8.95

PRIORITIES by Lynda Lyons 288 pp. Science fiction with
a twist. ISBN 0-941483-66-5 8.95

THEME FOR DIVERSE INSTRUMENTS by Jane Rule. 208
pp. Powerful romantic lesbian stories. ISBN 0-941483-63-0 8.95

LESBIAN QUERIES by Hertz & Ertman. 112 pp. The questions
you were too embarrassed to ask. ISBN 0-941483-67-3 8.95

CLUB 12 by Amanda Kyle Williams. 288 pp. Espionage thriller
featuring a lesbian agent! ISBN 0-941483-64-9 8.95

DEATH DOWN UNDER by Claire McNab. 240 pp. 3rd Det.
Insp. Carol Ashton mystery. ISBN 0-941483-39-8 9.95

MONTANA FEATHERS by Penny Hayes. 256 pp. Vivian and
Elizabeth find love in frontier Montana. ISBN 0-941483-61-4 8.95

CHESAPEAKE PROJECT by Phyllis Horn. 304 pp. Jessie &
Meredith in perilous adventure. ISBN 0-941483-58-4 8.95

LIFESTYLES by Jackie Calhoun. 224 pp. Contemporary Lesbian
lives and loves. ISBN 0-941483-57-6 9.95

VIRAGO by Karen Marie Christa Minns. 208 pp. Darsen has
chosen Ginny. ISBN 0-941483-56-8 8.95

WILDERNESS TREK by Dorothy Tell. 192 pp. Six women on
vacation learning "new" skills. ISBN 0-941483-60-6 8.95

MURDER BY THE BOOK by Pat Welch. 256 pp. A Helen
Black Mystery. First in a series. ISBN 0-941483-59-2 8.95

BERRIGAN by Vicki P. McConnell. 176 pp. Youthful Lesbian —
romantic, idealistic Berrigan. ISBN 0-941483-55-X 8.95

LESBIANS IN GERMANY by Lillian Faderman & B. Eriksson.
128 pp. Fiction, poetry, essays. ISBN 0-941483-62-2 8.95

THERE'S SOMETHING I'VE BEEN MEANING TO TELL
YOU Ed. by Loralee MacPike. 288 pp. Gay men and lesbians
coming out to their children. ISBN 0-941483-44-4 9.95
ISBN 0-941483-54-1 16.95

LIFTING BELLY by Gertrude Stein. Ed. by Rebecca Mark. 104
pp. Erotic poetry. ISBN 0-941483-51-7 8.95
ISBN 0-941483-53-3 14.95

ROSE PENSKI by Roz Perry. 192 pp. Adult lovers in a long-term
relationship. ISBN 0-941483-37-1 8.95

AFTER THE FIRE by Jane Rule. 256 pp. Warm, human novel by this incomparable author. ISBN 0-941483-45-2 8.95

SUE SLATE, PRIVATE EYE by Lee Lynch. 176 pp. The gay folk of Peacock Alley are *all cats*. ISBN 0-941483-52-5 8.95

CHRIS by Randy Salem. 224 pp. Golden oldie. Handsome Chris and her adventures. ISBN 0-941483-42-8 8.95

THREE WOMEN by March Hastings. 232 pp. Golden oldie. A triangle among wealthy sophisticates. ISBN 0-941483-43-6 8.95

RICE AND BEANS by Valeria Taylor. 232 pp. Love and romance on poverty row. ISBN 0-941483-41-X 8.95

PLEASURES by Robbi Sommers. 204 pp. Unprecedented eroticism. ISBN 0-941483-49-5 8.95

EDGEWISE by Camarin Grae. 372 pp. Spellbinding adventure. ISBN 0-941483-19-3 9.95

FATAL REUNION by Claire McNab. 224 pp. 2nd Det. Inspec. Carol Ashton mystery. ISBN 0-941483-40-1 8.95

KEEP TO ME STRANGER by Sarah Aldridge. 372 pp. Romance set in a department store dynasty. ISBN 0-941483-38-X 9.95

HEARTSCAPE by Sue Gambill. 204 pp. American lesbian in Portugal. ISBN 0-941483-33-9 8.95

IN THE BLOOD by Lauren Wright Douglas. 252 pp. Lesbian science fiction adventure fantasy ISBN 0-941483-22-3 8.95

THE BEE'S KISS by Shirley Verel. 216 pp. Delicate, delicious romance. ISBN 0-941483-36-3 8.95

RAGING MOTHER MOUNTAIN by Pat Emmerson. 264 pp. Furosa Firechild's adventures in Wonderland. ISBN 0-941483-35-5 8.95

IN EVERY PORT by Karin Kallmaker. 228 pp. Jessica's sexy, adventuresome travels. ISBN 0-941483-37-7 9.95

OF LOVE AND GLORY by Evelyn Kennedy. 192 pp. Exciting WWII romance. ISBN 0-941483-32-0 8.95

CLICKING STONES by Nancy Tyler Glenn. 288 pp. Love transcending time. ISBN 0-941483-31-2 9.95

SURVIVING SISTERS by Gail Pass. 252 pp. Powerful love story. ISBN 0-941483-16-9 8.95

SOUTH OF THE LINE by Catherine Ennis. 216 pp. Civil War adventure. ISBN 0-941483-29-0 8.95

WOMAN PLUS WOMAN by Dolores Klaich. 300 pp. Supurb Lesbian overview. ISBN 0-941483-28-2 9.95

SLOW DANCING AT MISS POLLY'S by Sheila Ortiz Taylor. 96 pp. Lesbian Poetry ISBN 0-941483-30-4 7.95

DOUBLE DAUGHTER by Vicki P. McConnell. 216 pp. A Nyla Wade Mystery, third in the series. ISBN 0-941483-26-6 8.95

HEAVY GILT by Delores Klaich. 192 pp. Lesbian detective/ disappearing homophobes/upper class gay society. ISBN 0-941483-25-8 8.95

THE FINER GRAIN by Denise Ohio. 216 pp. Brilliant young college lesbian novel. ISBN 0-941483-11-8 8.95

THE AMAZON TRAIL by Lee Lynch. 216 pp. Life, travel & lore of famous lesbian author. ISBN 0-941483-27-4 8.95

HIGH CONTRAST by Jessie Lattimore. 264 pp. Women of the Crystal Palace. ISBN 0-941483-17-7 8.95

OCTOBER OBSESSION by Meredith More. Josie's rich, secret Lesbian life. ISBN 0-941483-18-5 8.95

LESBIAN CROSSROADS by Ruth Baetz. 276 pp. Contemporary Lesbian lives. ISBN 0-941483-21-5 9.95

BEFORE STONEWALL: THE MAKING OF A GAY AND LESBIAN COMMUNITY by Andrea Weiss & Greta Schiller. 96 pp., 25 illus. ISBN 0-941483-20-7 7.95

WE WALK THE BACK OF THE TIGER by Patricia A. Murphy. 192 pp. Romantic Lesbian novel/beginning women's movement. ISBN 0-941483-13-4 8.95

SUNDAY'S CHILD by Joyce Bright. 216 pp. Lesbian athletics, at last the novel about sports. ISBN 0-941483-12-6 8.95

OSTEN'S BAY by Zenobia N. Vole. 204 pp. Sizzling adventure romance set on Bonaire. ISBN 0-941483-15-0 8.95

LESSONS IN MURDER by Claire McNab. 216 pp. 1st Det. Inspec. Carol Ashton mystery — erotic tension!. ISBN 0-941483-14-2 8.95

YELLOWTHROAT by Penny Hayes. 240 pp. Margarita, bandit, kidnaps Julia. ISBN 0-941483-10-X 8.95

SAPPHISTRY: THE BOOK OF LESBIAN SEXUALITY by Pat Califia. 3d edition, revised. 208 pp. ISBN 0-941483-24-X 8.95

CHERISHED LOVE by Evelyn Kennedy. 192 pp. Erotic Lesbian love story. ISBN 0-941483-08-8 9.95

LAST SEPTEMBER by Helen R. Hull. 208 pp. Six stories & a glorious novella. ISBN 0-941483-09-6 8.95

THE SECRET IN THE BIRD by Camarin Grae. 312 pp. Striking, psychological suspense novel. ISBN 0-941483-05-3 8.95

TO THE LIGHTNING by Catherine Ennis. 208 pp. Romantic Lesbian 'Robinson Crusoe' adventure. ISBN 0-941483-06-1 8.95

THE OTHER SIDE OF VENUS by Shirley Verel. 224 pp. Luminous, romantic love story. ISBN 0-941483-07-X 8.95

DREAMS AND SWORDS by Katherine V. Forrest. 192 pp. Romantic, erotic, imaginative stories. ISBN 0-941483-03-7 8.95

MEMORY BOARD by Jane Rule. 336 pp. Memorable novel about an aging Lesbian couple. ISBN 0-941483-02-9 9.95

THE ALWAYS ANONYMOUS BEAST by Lauren Wright Douglas. 224 pp. A Caitlin Reece mystery. First in a series. ISBN 0-941483-04-5 8.95

SEARCHING FOR SPRING by Patricia A. Murphy. 224 pp. Novel about the recovery of love. ISBN 0-941483-00-2 8.95

DUSTY'S QUEEN OF HEARTS DINER by Lee Lynch. 240 pp. Romantic blue-collar novel. ISBN 0-941483-01-0 8.95

PARENTS MATTER by Ann Muller. 240 pp. Parents' relationships with Lesbian daughters and gay sons. ISBN 0-930044-91-6 9.95

THE PEARLS by Shelley Smith. 176 pp. Passion and fun in the Caribbean sun. ISBN 0-930044-93-2 7.95

MAGDALENA by Sarah Aldridge. 352 pp. Epic Lesbian novel set on three continents. ISBN 0-930044-99-1 8.95

THE BLACK AND WHITE OF IT by Ann Allen Shockley. 144 pp. Short stories. ISBN 0-930044-96-7 7.95

SAY JESUS AND COME TO ME by Ann Allen Shockley. 288 pp. Contemporary romance. ISBN 0-930044-98-3 8.95

LOVING HER by Ann Allen Shockley. 192 pp. Romantic love story. ISBN 0-930044-97-5 7.95

MURDER AT THE NIGHTWOOD BAR by Katherine V. Forrest. 240 pp. A Kate Delafield mystery. Second in a series. ISBN 0-930044-92-4 9.95

ZOE'S BOOK by Gail Pass. 224 pp. Passionate, obsessive love story. ISBN 0-930044-95-9 7.95

WINGED DANCER by Camarin Grae. 228 pp. Erotic Lesbian adventure story. ISBN 0-930044-88-6 8.95

PAZ by Camarin Grae. 336 pp. Romantic Lesbian adventurer with the power to change the world. ISBN 0-930044-89-4 8.95

SOUL SNATCHER by Camarin Grae. 224 pp. A puzzle, an adventure, a mystery — Lesbian romance. ISBN 0-930044-90-8 8.95

THE LOVE OF GOOD WOMEN by Isabel Miller. 224 pp. Long-awaited new novel by the author of the beloved *Patience and Sarah.* ISBN 0-930044-81-9 8.95

THE HOUSE AT PELHAM FALLS by Brenda Weathers. 240 pp. Suspenseful Lesbian ghost story. ISBN 0-930044-79-7 7.95

HOME IN YOUR HANDS by Lee Lynch. 240 pp. More stories from the author of *Old Dyke Tales.* ISBN 0-930044-80-0 7.95

EACH HAND A MAP by Anita Skeen. 112 pp. Real-life poems that touch us all. ISBN 0-930044-82-7 6.95

SURPLUS by Sylvia Stevenson. 342 pp. A classic early Lesbian novel. ISBN 0-930044-78-9 7.95

PEMBROKE PARK by Michelle Martin. 256 pp. Derring-do and daring romance in Regency England. ISBN 0-930044-77-0 7.95

THE LONG TRAIL by Penny Hayes. 248 pp. Vivid adventures of two women in love in the old west. ISBN 0-930044-76-2 8.95

HORIZON OF THE HEART by Shelley Smith. 192 pp. Hot romance in summertime New England. ISBN 0-930044-75-4 7.95

AN EMERGENCE OF GREEN by Katherine V. Forrest. 288 pp. Powerful novel of sexual discovery. ISBN 0-930044-69-X 9.95

THE LESBIAN PERIODICALS INDEX edited by Claire Potter. 432 pp. Author & subject index. ISBN 0-930044-74-6 29.95

DESERT OF THE HEART by Jane Rule. 224 pp. A classic; basis for the movie *Desert Hearts.* ISBN 0-930044-73-8 9.95

SPRING FORWARD/FALL BACK by Sheila Ortiz Taylor. 288 pp. Literary novel of timeless love. ISBN 0-930044-70-3 7.95

FOR KEEPS by Elisabeth Nonas. 144 pp. Contemporary novel about losing and finding love. ISBN 0-930044-71-1 7.95

TORCHLIGHT TO VALHALLA by Gale Wilhelm. 128 pp. Classic novel by a great Lesbian writer. ISBN 0-930044-68-1 7.95

LESBIAN NUNS: BREAKING SILENCE edited by Rosemary Curb and Nancy Manahan. 432 pp. Unprecedented autobiographies of religious life. ISBN 0-930044-62-2 9.95

THE SWASHBUCKLER by Lee Lynch. 288 pp. Colorful novel set in Greenwich Village in the sixties. ISBN 0-930044-66-5 8.95

MISFORTUNE'S FRIEND by Sarah Aldridge. 320 pp. Historical Lesbian novel set on two continents. ISBN 0-930044-67-3 7.95

A STUDIO OF ONE'S OWN by Ann Stokes. Edited by Dolores Klaich. 128 pp. Autobiography. ISBN 0-930044-64-9 7.95

SEX VARIANT WOMEN IN LITERATURE by Jeannette Howard Foster. 448 pp. Literary history. ISBN 0-930044-65-7 8.95

A HOT-EYED MODERATE by Jane Rule. 252 pp. Hard-hitting essays on gay life; writing; art. ISBN 0-930044-57-6 7.95

INLAND PASSAGE AND OTHER STORIES by Jane Rule. 288 pp. Wide-ranging new collection. ISBN 0-930044-56-8 7.95

WE TOO ARE DRIFTING by Gale Wilhelm. 128 pp. Timeless Lesbian novel, a masterpiece. ISBN 0-930044-61-4 6.95

AMATEUR CITY by Katherine V. Forrest. 224 pp. A Kate Delafield mystery. First in a series. ISBN 0-930044-55-X 9.95

THE SOPHIE HOROWITZ STORY by Sarah Schulman. 176 pp. Engaging novel of madcap intrigue. ISBN 0-930044-54-1 7.95

THE YOUNG IN ONE ANOTHER'S ARMS by Jane Rule. 224 pp. Classic Jane Rule. ISBN 0-930044-53-3 9.95

THE BURNTON WIDOWS by Vickie P. McConnell. 272 pp. A Nyla Wade mystery, second in the series. ISBN 0-930044-52-5 9.95

OLD DYKE TALES by Lee Lynch. 224 pp. Extraordinary stories of our diverse Lesbian lives. ISBN 0-930044-51-7 8.95

DAUGHTERS OF A CORAL DAWN by Katherine V. Forrest. 240 pp. Novel set in a Lesbian new world. ISBN 0-930044-50-9 8.95

AGAINST THE SEASON by Jane Rule. 224 pp. Luminous, complex novel of interrelationships. ISBN 0-930044-48-7 8.95

LOVERS IN THE PRESENT AFTERNOON by Kathleen Fleming. 288 pp. A novel about recovery and growth. ISBN 0-930044-46-0 8.95

TOOTHPICK HOUSE by Lee Lynch. 264 pp. Love between two Lesbians of different classes. ISBN 0-930044-45-2 7.95

MADAME AURORA by Sarah Aldridge. 256 pp. Historical novel featuring a charismatic "seer." ISBN 0-930044-44-4 7.95

CURIOUS WINE by Katherine V. Forrest. 176 pp. Passionate Lesbian love story, a best-seller. ISBN 0-930044-43-6 8.95

BLACK LESBIAN IN WHITE AMERICA by Anita Cornwell. 141 pp. Stories, essays, autobiography. ISBN 0-930044-41-X 7.95

CONTRACT WITH THE WORLD by Jane Rule. 340 pp. Powerful, panoramic novel of gay life. ISBN 0-930044-28-2 9.95

MRS. PORTER'S LETTER by Vicki P. McConnell. 224 pp. The first Nyla Wade mystery. ISBN 0-930044-29-0 7.95

TO THE CLEVELAND STATION by Carol Anne Douglas. 192 pp. Interracial Lesbian love story. ISBN 0-930044-27-4 6.95

THE NESTING PLACE by Sarah Aldridge. 224 pp. A three-woman triangle — love conquers all! ISBN 0-930044-26-6 7.95

THIS IS NOT FOR YOU by Jane Rule. 284 pp. A letter to a beloved is also an intricate novel. ISBN 0-930044-25-8 8.95

FAULTLINE by Sheila Ortiz Taylor. 140 pp. Warm, funny, literate story of a startling family. ISBN 0-930044-24-X 6.95

ANNA'S COUNTRY by Elizabeth Lang. 208 pp. A woman finds her Lesbian identity. ISBN 0-930044-19-3 8.95

These are just a few of the many Naiad Press titles — we are the oldest and largest lesbian/feminist publishing company in the world. Please request a complete catalog. We offer personal service; we encourage and welcome direct mail orders from individuals who have limited access to bookstores carrying our publications.